VISTAS, VICES, & VALENTINES

A CAMPER AND CRIMINALS COZY MYSTERY SERIES

TONYA KAPPES

PREVIEW

"The car is running!" she gasped and reached down to pick up a large metal remote control–looking thing with a red and a green button. She hit the red button, and the car started to descend.

I hurried over to the garage door, where I punched the garage-door opener to let some air into the garage because I knew carbon monoxide was poisonous.

"I can't believe Bobby Ray would keep a car running," I said to Felicity and turned back around to watch the tires of the car land on the cement floor of the garage.

"What?" she asked when she noticed the look on my face.

I licked my lips and said, "I think Kirby found Rick." My eyes fixed upon Rick's lifeless body in the back seat of Felicity's car. As if in slow motion, my eyes took in Felicity's hand dropping the metal remote control onto the garage's cement floor.

GET FREE BOOKS

Join Tonya's newsletter.
See all of Tonya's books.
Find all these links on Tonya's website, Tonyakappes.com.

CHAPTER 1

"This is ridiculous," Hank grumbled under his breath. His green eyes squinted as they shifted left to right, taking in the other gentlemen who were standing in line with him. He looked at me.

Just smile through it, I told myself and tried to keep my shaky arms extended into a T formation.

My jaw tensed. My teeth gritted in a forced thin smile.

"This was your idea." Hank had no problem making sure I recalled how much fun I'd thought it was going to be to offer free dance lessons to the guests of Happy Trails Campground during the week of Valentine's Day since the International Dance Company was holding their big competition in Normal, Kentucky. "I'm just being dragged along." He stretched his neck side to side like we were about to be a tag team in a wrestling match.

I'd gotten Corie Sadek's information from Queenie, who was our local Jazzercise instructor. Queenie was really involved in dance, and there was a dance class not too far from us in the neighboring town of Beattyville, Kentucky.

Corie and her dance partner, Ricky, were more than happy

to take my money to teach a few lessons to get us up to speed for Valentine's Day. Plus, she'd mentioned it would give them some practice for the dance competition that was being hosted at the Train Station Motel.

Of course, I'd seen those famous dance-competition shows on television, but I'd not realized just how much they had given the dance industry until it came to the National Forest Park Committee's desk that there'd been a permit filed to host the huge event. That was when I started to look into the industry, and boy, there was some big money to be made if you were really good at the craft.

"You keep reminding me it's my idea." I sucked in a deep breath and focused on not shaking when I saw the instructors walking down the line, correcting everyone's posture.

The Old Train Station Motel had an old barn on the property that'd been converted to an events center. It'd become a popular destination for weddings—not a big surprise since the motel had gorgeous views of not only the sunrise but the sunset, with the grandiose Daniel Boone National Forest as the backdrop.

"For a few basic formations…" The five-foot-seven instructor walked around like a breeze. She had long blond hair that swayed atop a mesh red dress over matching leggings as she flitted from couple to couple, as did Ricky.

Corie seemed to work with the men, and Ricky worked with the ladies. Both had slight accents that told me they weren't from America, but I could tell by the way they spoke slowly and precisely that they were really trying to cover it up.

Hank and I had already established who'd be the lead dancer and who'd be the follower. Hank was the leader in our case because in my head, I had been playing like the movie *Dirty Dancing* without the famous water scene, though I did have the unruly curly hair like Baby.

I snickered at the thought of Hank and me standing in the large stream off Red Fox Trail with me lifted above his head while I pretend to soar like an eagle before tumbling into the water, like Baby and Johnny from the movie.

Fat chance.

"Very nice." Corie ran a slim finger down my arm, tracing a path to Hank's shoulder before tapping it. "You will hold your partner by karate chopping your right hand underneath her armpit," she instructed the group and used Hank to demonstrate.

She smiled and moved to Bobby Ray Bond and Abby Fawn Bond, his wife.

Corie slightly wrinkled her nose and gestured for Bobby Ray to really get up under Abby's armpit. I could tell Bobby Ray was really trying his best, even on his appearance. He wasn't wearing his baseball hat that usually covered most of his loose blond curls. They were free-flowing.

Abby giggled, her core sunk in. She looked so cute with her long brown hair free from her usual ponytail. It lay down her back in ringlets.

"I'm ticklish." Abby laughed some more before she curled her lips in, trying to force a serious face when Corie didn't find it a bit amusing. "But we can try again."

"Now cup your hands around your partner's shoulder blade. You can hold your partner's right hand as high as his or her eye level without raising their shoulder." Corie continued to walk around and fix the other dance partners' forms. "Ricky, please show Kirby how to properly hold Felicity." She spoke of Kirby and Felicity Marshall, a young couple who were guests of Happy Trails and had signed up for the class through the campground website.

Ricky glided his way across the old barn floor, sweeping Felicity into his arms.

"I know how to hold her, buddy." Kirby's tone was stiff.

"I'm sure you do, but in this case, you treat her like the fine delicate rose she is." Ricky gave her a swarmy smile that left a bad taste in my mouth.

Kirby took a hard step back. His brows hooded his eyes, never once giving any sort of acknowledgment to the instructions Ricky was giving him about his dance form. Instead, Ricky made his way over to the large barn windows, where the thick velvet drapes had helped transform the venue into an elegant ballroom.

The lights had been temporarily changed to tiered crystal chandeliers that glistened in the soft light. The morning sun filtered through the windows, hitting the chandeliers just right to create little sparks all over the interior of the barn in a mirror-ball effect.

There was a balcony where the brides loved to throw their bouquets to the eager single ladies below but not this week. This week, the live band and orchestra would call it home, accompanying the dancers on their quest to win the championship.

Hank tugged me in a little closer.

"Keep your eyes on me. Not them." He bent down and kissed my nose.

"This is kinda nice." I shrugged while keeping one hand on the top of Hank's bicep with the other cradled in his hand.

"Straighten up, Bobby Ray." Abby did her best to get Bobby Ray on board, but he kept wiggling his hips like he was doing some sort of salsa dance, making Abby belt out into more laughter.

"This basic footwork step is simple and perfect for beginners like all of us." Corie had brought her thin hands together in front of her, making her way over to Hank. She tapped him on the shoulder. "Excuse me. Can I borrow him?"

"I guess," I groaned with a snarl and furrowed brows, knowing exactly how Kirby must've felt.

The raised brows of Queenie French, Dottie Swaggert, and Betts Hager didn't go unnoticed.

The three of them didn't have dance partners for the class, so they'd been switching off.

Betts had her bangs styled to the side to complement her wavy brown hair. Dottie must've left her pink sponge curlers in a little too long this morning because her red hair was so tight to her head.

"You're going to start with your left foot, taking a step to the left." Corie stood tall, as Hank had put one hand in her pit and the other around her.

I gave the ladies a hard look before I walked over to them.

"I'm not as cute as him, but I guess I can take on your two left feet," Dottie said through a snicker before she took my hands in hers.

Betts and Queenie both laughed.

"Here we go," Corie said and gave a slight nod to Hank. "Left foot, two steps, in time with my count." She gave him instructions. "One, two, three." She was soft-spoken. "Four, five, six."

They stopped right on the edge of the dance floor before they ran into the audience part of the room.

Every dining table was perfectly spaced and already set as if the competition was right now and not starting tonight. The four-day extravaganza was highly anticipated, and you were lucky if you scored a ticket to the event. Seeing as I was on the committee, I scored tickets for myself and all of my friends.

The tables had white tablecloths, napkins puffed into wineglasses, and perfectly polished and spaced silverware as well as gold-edged china place settings. The flower centerpieces were fresh and gave the entire barn a nice scent.

"Very good." Corie winked at Hank and turned back to the

class. "Please." She gestured for me to step back into place with him.

"Aww. I thought we had chemistry," Dottie said and let go.

"I'm a good student." Hank wiggled his brows.

"Now you like the class?" I asked with a wry brow.

"Let's take a look at the followers' footwork. We're going to start with the right foot, taking a step to the right." She looked side to side, catching the eyes of the followers, including me. "You will do the same count: one, two, three." She pointed to her feet. "Now come back the other way. Four, five, six."

Hank led with his left while I followed with my right for two steps and then back.

"Very nice." Corie was pleased. "Stay in position while I get the music on."

Corie gracefully swept across the floor to talk to Ricky—or more like fuss at Ricky. He had his chin down and bent toward her neck as if he didn't want us to see them arguing.

"You're a playboy, and it'll get you nowhere." There was a bite in Corie's voice.

Ricky gave her a squinted look.

"One of these days, you're going to get your due, but for now, if you screw up this opportunity for me, for us..." She cleared her throat and gave a quick glance over her shoulder at us. We were all watching and waiting for her, frozen in our positions. "Put it this way—I won't let you screw this up for me."

She picked her phone up from the windowsill and slid her finger up the screen. "We will do this step until we have all mastered it," she said with a fake smile as the music started.

"One, two, three." I mouthed the count and looked down. "Four, five, six."

"Followers, look into your leader's eyes, not at your feet." Her voice boomed over the music. She and Ricky kept to the beat in perfect time.

Dottie fumbled around the dance floor with Betts. Queenie laughed the whole time.

"Leaders, shoulders away from the ears and back. Good posture. How do you lead with bad form? You don't." Corie continued to instruct, not realizing everyone in class was somewhat lost.

She and Ricky stood in the middle of the circle of couples. Corie placed one hand on her stomach and pretended to pull up a string above her head with the other in order to show off her good form, then she used her hands on Ricky's body to properly demonstrate.

Ricky took Corie into his arms and swept her across the floor next to Kirby and Felicity.

"Feel the music," Corie told them. "This is someone you love, no?" she asked them.

It was Kirby and Felicity's five-year wedding anniversary. I only knew because they'd gotten the anniversary-gift basket add-on for the bungalow they'd rented for the week of Valentine's Day.

"Of course I love her." Kirby snorted while rolling his eyes.

"You don't act like it," Felicity said with a voice that didn't sound like she was teasing and smacked his arm.

"Why did you do that?" Kirby questioned his wife as he glared and jerked away from her.

"Because you aren't doing this for us." Felicity sniffed, bringing her hand up to her nose.

"I am doing this for you," Kirby spat. "I sure ain't doing it for me. I should be working on the car."

"Fine." Felicity stomped even farther away from him. "Go work on your stupid car, and don't worry about our marriage. I should've listened to my dad and left you a long time ago. You..." She hesitated. "You're worthless!"

"Why do you have to always get on me like that?" Kirby

hurried out of the barn behind her, leaving us all standing there in silence other than the music playing in the background.

"I know the feeling, honey." Abby thought she was being funny. By the way Bobby Ray reacted, I could tell something was wrong. "Oh, stop it." Abby brought him closer to her. "You are a workaholic when it comes to cars."

"It's my job, Abby." Bobby Ray let go of her hands. "I'm a mechanic. And you sure like to spend money."

Abby's face reddened.

"Then could you possibly help out Kirby and Felicity with their car problems?" Corie injected herself when the tension in the room became very strong.

"I bet they'd be more appreciative," Bobby Ray said in acceptance but aimed his words at Abby. "I'm done for the day. I've got to get to work anyways." He walked away, throwing a hand behind him.

"'The day?" Abby yelled after him. "We just started." She threw her hands up in the air as her jaw dropped. As she turned her head to look at me, her eyes grew bigger and bigger. "Can you believe him?" Abby asked our group of friends.

"This was supposed to be fun," Queenie said. "Not get everyone upset. Maybe I was wrong in suggesting Corie come to teach, but it's a month of love, and the competition is hosted in Normal this year."

"It is a good idea," I confirmed to her so she wouldn't feel bad. "I love offering classes to my guests, and I hope they go and watch the competition."

"Unbelievable." Abby gasped, apparently upset we didn't agree with her. She bolted out the door.

"What shall we do?" Corie looked at me for answers.

"I think we can continue." I pinched a smile, looking around at the other couples as well as Betts, Queenie, and Dottie. They all agreed.

"Very good. Back to the starter position, please." Corie continued with the counting. "One, two, three." She paused and gave one hard nod. "Four, five, six."

"What do you think that was about?" I asked Hank.

"Bobby Ray or the other couple?" He pulled me closer.

"I have no idea. Something is in the air." I felt him bring me even closer, so I held on.

"Love." He picked me up and swung me around. "Love is in the air."

"No! No!" Corie called from across the room. "That's not a move, and it's certainly not what anyone else should be doing."

It was like Hank had started a trend. All the couples were twirling each other around, sending Corie into an all-out tizzy.

I threw my head back and laughed.

Something was definitely in the air.

CHAPTER 2

The undeniable chill that ran along my arms and found its way down my spine didn't come from the last of the winter weather hanging around the Daniel Boone National Forest—it wasn't unusual for Mother Nature's mood swings to take the temperature from twenty degrees to seventy degrees during the months before springtime.

The chill came after I heard Felicity and Kirby screaming at each other at the top of their lungs in the parking lot of the Old Train Station Motel. The echo bounced off the trees and mountains surrounding the motel, which didn't help matters.

"Gracious me." Corie floated from inside the barn, gripping her radio in one hand and her bag in the other. Ricky was on his way up to the motel with the other items they'd brought, stopping briefly to talk to another dancer. "I can tell by the way couples hold themselves during dance classes where they are in their relationship."

"Really?" I found that to be very interesting.

"Oh yes. The way they touch each other. Their eyes." She nodded, lifting both brows. "You two have the eyes of deep-soul love." Her finger swung around to point to the ushers. "Those two have issues."

"That's probably why they had all them love baskets ordered," Dottie chimed in. Smoke rolled out of her mouth as she puffed away on the cigarette. She was sitting on top of one of the picnic tables, legs crossed, swinging the top leg.

"They better not spill the wax off them candles either"—she brought the cigarette hand up to her face, squinted, and took notice of her nails—"'cause I just got Glenda to do my nails, and I ain't gonna be scraping no dried wax off them wood floors."

Corie's lips clamped together as she appeared to swallow a laugh.

"We've got insurance." I shrugged and turned to Corie. "Dottie Swaggert is the manager of Happy Trails." I took a moment to properly introduce them since Corie wasn't sure who was a guest of the campground versus a local or an employee.

At the beginning of every year, I budgeted for special events like dance classes for guests as well as members of the community. Our small town of Normal, set in the middle of the Daniel Boone National Forest, had become a tourist town mainly based around hiking, kayaking, camping, and cave exploring.

Offering special events allowed the community to get involved with tourists on a fun level. Plus, the locals were able to offer their services—like Betts was the owner of the local laundromat, the Laundry Club. It was a win for everyone involved.

"It's very nice to meet all of you," Corie said. "But I have to get back to the barn. It's almost rehearsal time for me and Ricky. Four nights of glorious dancing for the town, but the judges will be watching our every step."

"That's exciting," Betts said with a smile. "I've never been to a dance competition, but I've seen them on television."

"Competitions have gotten very crowded since those dancing competition shows started on television," Corie said just as I watched Henry Bryant pull up next to the curb in his car. He'd been kind enough to offer Felicity and Kirby a ride to the motel after they couldn't get their car started.

I'd already left when Henry called me, and I told him the campground insurance would cover his driving them to the motel for the lesson. Felicity and Kirby must've made an agreement to have him pick them up too.

Felicity and Kirby got into the car and Henry got out, leaving them in the back. By the way their heads were bobbing back and forth, along with their mouths running, they were still arguing once they got into the car.

"I'm sorry to interrupt," he said when he walked up to us. The smile on his face exposed his missing two front teeth. His scraggly hair stuck out every which way from his baseball cap. "Mae, do you want me to get all those paper hearts out of storage when I get back to Happy Trails?" he asked.

"It's the month of love, ain't it?" Dottie asked, with her question directed at Corie. She then bent down to snuff out her cigarette on a concrete slab before she stuck the butt in her jeans pocket.

There was nothing more disgusting than seeing cigarette butts lying all over the Daniel Boone National Forest. Luckily, Dottie felt the same way. She was always picking up other people's cigarette butts.

"Dottie." Henry blinked with zero emotion on his face. "You ain't my boss no more. So don't tell me what to do." Henry seemed to have had his limits with Dottie's bossing the fella around after all these years of working with her.

"Oh dear." Corie's posture lifted. "You two are fireballs. Why aren't you taking my class Mae is offering?" Corie directed her question at Henry. "We do need one more dance partner." She was referring to Betts, Dottie, and Queenie taking turns dancing with each other in class.

"Fireballs?" Dottie spat.

"Huh?" Henry questioned.

"You two have amazing chemistry, and that makes a great dance couple." Corie nearly caused me to nearly pee my pants from giggling, which I couldn't seem to stop before it turned into an all-out belly laugh. "Dottie needs a dance partner."

"Those two?" I snorted out through the tears streaming down my face.

"Oh yeah." Corie's eyes grew, her head nodded, and she looked like she'd just discovered the perfect dance couple. "You two aren't..."

"Aren't what?" Dottie took a deep breath.

I winced in anticipation of what was going to come out of Corie's mouth.

"An item?" Corie questioned. "A couple?"

There it was.

I gulped.

"Me and her?" Henry pulled off his John Deere cap and smacked it down on his knee, cackling. "Me and her?" he asked again.

Henry laughed, and the tension that started at Dottie's toes and radiated up her body was visible. "I wouldn't have Henry Bryant as no boyfriend. Why, he's as useless as a milk bucket underneath a bull." She jerked the cigarette case out the front pocket of her jeans, unsnapped it, and got another cigarette out.

"Yeah, yeah." Henry couldn't stop laughing. "Kissing her would be like licking an ashtray."

Dottie's jaw dropped. Her eyes grew big, and I could have sworn her head was about to spin off her shoulders.

"Please get the decorations out." I had to stop this wild conversation before Henry lost his life, because Dottie's face was as red as the curly hair on her head.

Henry looked at Corie one last time and just couldn't help

himself. He started laughing all over again until he was finally able to say, "Mae, before I forget, I just saw Bobby Ray, and he asked if he and Abby could stop by the campground and grab some firewood. I told him that'd be alright." He put his hat back on his head. "It is alright, ain't it?"

"It's fine." I gave a little head tilt to Dottie to stir the pot a little. "Maybe Dottie wants a ride back with you."

"You better get on out of here!" Dottie shook the lit cigarette at him. "You, little missy, better straighten up," she told me.

"I didn't mean to intrude, but there's something there." Corie nodded.

"I..." Dottie opened her mouth.

I shut her down. "Thank you so much. Even though they aren't a couple, they might consider entering since there's a one-hundred-dollar cash prize." I acted as though I didn't see Dottie's face light up when I mentioned the money.

Or any prize at all. Dottie was what you'd call very competitive. So much so, she didn't care what the prize was—if there was a prize, she'd enter. She did the same thing when the town of Normal would host beauty contests for people in her age range.

Two ladies in dance uniforms walked past us as they left the motel restaurant. Both of them made eye contact with Corie.

Corie glanced at them but turned her attention back to us.

"You two could just try it out and see if you're compatible as dance partners." Corie shrugged. She turned toward the car. Ricky motioned for her to join. "I'd think about it, because I'm the instructor, and trust me when I say not one couple in there has chemistry like you and Henry."

"Uh..." I muttered.

"Not even you and Hank, though you two are very compatible. These two..." Corie tsked and shook her head. She let go of a long sigh. "I've got to go. I'll see you two—possibly three—later." She winked.

"Maybe they aren't romantically involved," I suggested and jerked around when I heard some yelling.

Kirby and Felicity got our attention again as Felicity slammed the car door.

"But maybe not those two," Corie said before she excused herself, leaving me and Dottie looking down the campground toward the far end of the lake where the bungalows were located.

"She needs to work on her own chemistry with Ricky. They are on opposite sides of the romance street." Dottie made a really good observation about the two. "They ain't no Rita Hayworth and Fred Astaire."

"My oh my, do I need to see if we got a camper open?" Dottie questioned when the bungalow door opened and Felicity swung out some sort of big bag, aiming at Kirby.

Kirby threw his arms over his head and said a few choice words that I could make out that I'd never repeat.

"I reckon you better get on back to the campground and all." Dottie gave me the side-eye.

"You're on duty, not me." I reminded her how it was her shift to work in the office and any disturbances were on her dime.

"I'll kick them out." She playacted like she was big and bad, but she was just an old softie.

"No, you won't." I groaned. "Fine. I'll go on back. I need to get Fifi anyway."

"Poor Fifi." Dottie shook her head. "You're using that poor baby to go with you as a buffer because she's too cute for anyone not to soften when they pet her."

Felicity came back over to us. "I'm sorry to bother you," she said, "but do you think you could give me a ride back to the main campground? I won't go anywhere with him right now."

"I guess I can, if you're sure." I didn't want to cause any troubles for them.

"Come on, Felicity." Kirby had gotten out of the car and called for her from over the hood, his arms rested on top with his hands folded together. "Henry came all this way. I'm sorry, baby. We can talk about it in the car."

"Why don't you go with him?" I suggested. "Not even Hank likes the dance lessons, but he is doing them for me."

"And it's heart week and all." Dottie nodded.

Felicity sighed. Her lips melted into a faltering grin.

"I guess I can give him another chance." She shook her head. "I wonder how many chances someone should get."

"As many as it takes to get it right," I told her, thinking about how much I'd messed up my life until the good people of Normal had embraced me and given me the one chance it took to get my life back on track.

"You're right. Plus, I really want to make this work with Kirby." Her grin turned into a big smile. "I'll see you two later."

"You sure will," I said.

Dottie and I waved her off.

"They ain't gonna make it," Dottie said under her breath.

CHAPTER 3

Happy Trails Campground was a beautiful campground that Dottie, Henry, and I had worked so hard over the past few years to get back into tip-top shape after I'd inherited the place from my Ponzi-scheming now-dead ex-husband.

It was one thing I was actually thankful for. I had never intended on staying in Normal, much less being the owner of a campground. I'd fallen in love with the people and the Daniel Boone National Forest. It was a truly magical and special place here.

Most days, I loved to sit down in one of the Adirondack chairs around the campground to relax—it might take a while, but you were guaranteed to see some sort of bird or little critter who had made their home in the campground scurry by the chair. Of course, when you heard something scatter in the darkness of the night, it could be a little frightening, thanks to the active nightlife of nocturnal animals. But the forest was an amazing place to fall asleep and let your dreams fall over you, which made me wonder why the magic wasn't working on Kirby and Felicity.

Many couples came to Happy Trails for a romantic getaway. Every month, we hosted a party at Happy Trails for not only our guests but the entire community. Dottie and I had been doing this for so long that we'd seen couples with problems in their relationship leave without an ounce of stress, a chemistry between them reignited. We loved to see them come back for their yearly relationship refresh, and that was one reason I was hosting the Valentine's dance this year.

I had parked my car on the concrete pad in front of my campervan. Instead of pulling the camper out and driving it everywhere, which was costly and time-consuming, I'd bought a little car from Joel down at Grassel's Garage. It was just a simple little four-door Ford and did the job I needed it to do—got me to and from town.

Out of the corner of my eye, I noticed something to the left.

Clothes were flying out of the bungalow Kirby and Felicity had rented at record speed, with a follow-up duffle bag smacking Kirby in the face. Kirby picked up the clothes and tried to stuff them in the bag. He didn't get too much picked up before he started throw them back on the ground. His emotions were escalating, and he needed to be stopped.

Hank must've thought so too, because he'd emerged from his camper, which was a couple down from mine. He looked at me and I held up my hand.

"I'm getting Fifi. Hold on." The awning of my campervan was out. I put my phone on the picnic table I kept under there to stay shielded from precipitation and opened my small camper door.

Fifi, my toy poodle, was eagerly waiting for me. Her nails clicked on the luxurious vinyl flooring.

"Hey, sweet girl." She didn't need her leash during the day like she did at night. The daytime critters living in and around the woods didn't see Fifi as food like the nighttime animals did. "Come on."

I reached out and picked her up from the doorway of the camper, placing her down on the outdoor rug before she scampered off in Hank's camper's direction.

Fifi was trained to know that if Chester, Hank's dog, wasn't with me, then we would be going to let him out. Hank and Chester were already outside, standing on the road that led around the campground and waiting on us.

Fifi danced around Chester, and he stood still as a statue until he jumped up on his hind legs and scampered off with Fifi running behind him.

"What do you think we need to do about them?" Hank threw his chin toward the bungalow where Kirby was still letting go of anger.

"Not that it's any of our business what they are fighting about, but it is my business to keep the peace in the campground." I tried not to stare at the other people who'd come from inside their campers to see what all the fussing was about.

Hank agreed.

"Since you're ex-sheriff, maybe you can handle it." Hank's expertise came in handy for me even though he was now a private investigator between jobs. "Those two I'll handle." I looked back to the campground office, where Bobby Ray and Abby were discussing whatever disagreement they were having.

"How's it going?" Hank asked Kirby and bent down to pick up what looked to be stray tools, like wrenches and pliers.

"As you can see, Felicity has decided to throw me and my tool bag out of the cabin." Kirby shook a fist in the air toward the bungalow.

Felicity jerked the curtains of the window closed.

"Is there something I can help you figure out?" Hank asked. "I mean, Mae and I would like to make sure you two have a good stay, and right now, it's not looking that way."

"I appreciate it. But Felicity really wanted to go hiking over on Cherokee today, and I've got something going on with the engine. I was supposed to get it serviced before we left and, well—" He sighed and said, "Ended up that I lied and didn't do it. The cost of the trip took more money than I'd budgeted."

"Don't you let him fool you!" Felicity had swung the door open, and she stood in the doorway. "I've been saving for this trip for months because the reservations were so booked. He was supposed to be saving for the car to get fixed, and now that it's broke down"—she shook her finger at the car —"*again*," she emphasized, "I knew he lied. Always lying to me!"

"Let me go talk to her," I suggested and left Hank standing there with Kirby.

Before I walked inside the bungalow, I made sure to scan the campground for Fifi and Chester. They were running from camper to camper not only to get a few good scratches but to beg for food.

"Kirby tells me you want to go hiking in Cherokee today." I stepped inside. "Well, it just so happens that tomorrow morning, I'm going to be checking out a new trail."

"That sounds fun." She walked over to the refrigerator, leaving me at the door. "Do you want something to drink? Water? Coke?"

"I'll take a bottled water if you've got it, and we can sit on the deck if you want while the guys figure out the car." It was my way of getting her out of her head and letting her know everything was casual and would all work out. "I'll meet you outside."

I walked through the small bungalow and unlocked the sliding glass door that opened out onto the deck. This particular bungalow had the best deck that jutted over the hillside like the prow of a ship. The deck had the best views of the forest and the daily morning sunrises. The light, warm breeze caused the flag attached to one of the deck's rails to slap and pull against the rope of its pole, reminding me of a well-washed sheet on a clothesline.

I was lost in thought when I heard Felicity saying something to me while walking through the sliding door. "I'm sorry," I apologized. "I was just thinking about the first time I saw this view."

"It is nice." Felicity smiled, softening her hard exterior. "I just wished Kirby and I could enjoy it like I thought we were going to."

"I have a solution for everyone." I took my phone out and dialed Bobby Ray. "My brother is the local mechanic. He can get your car to the gas station and work on it while I take you with me on the trail in the morning."

"You'd do that for us?" she asked and handed me the bottle of water.

"Of course. I'd do anything for my guests to enjoy themselves." Almost anything. "Tonight, I will buy the two of you supper at the Red Barn. In fact, Hank and I will join you."

I held a finger up when Bobby Ray answered.

"Hey." I didn't let on to Felicity that he answered by asking me if I could talk some sense into Abby. "One of our guests is having car trouble. Do you think you could look at the engine and see if you can help him out?"

Bobby Ray moaned.

"Then, tonight, I thought it would be fun for the six of us to go eat at the Red Barn. On me." The "on me" part did stop him from babbling on the other end of the phone.

"On you?" he asked.

"Yes. And is Abby still up there with you?" I asked, knowing she had to work the afternoon shift at the Normal Public Library.

"Yep." By the way he answered, I knew they still weren't in agreement about whatever they were fighting about.

"Why don't you tell her to come on down with you," I

suggested even though I knew she had to get to work at some point.

"I reckon we can." Bobby Ray's end of the phone went silent. I pulled the phone away from my ear and noticed he'd just hung up without saying goodbye.

"I've been on your reservation waiting list for a while." Felicity lifted her eyes to the sunshine and inhaled deeply. "I was so happy to get the email from Dottie letting me know there was a cancellation." She opened her eyes and looked down at her fingers as they fiddled with a hangnail. "Kirby said it was a bad time to go on a trip, but I insisted."

"Because of the car?" I questioned if that was the reason Kirby had thought it was a bad time.

"No. The car just piled on top. We were actually going to let our families know we were separating." Her words brought a surprised expression to my face, and she noticed. "Yeah. I guess you're wondering why even bother or why I would get the baskets of goodies."

"It's none of my business." I leaned slightly forward in the chair with my hands tucked between my knees. "I don't have room to talk. Hank, my boyfriend—" I waited for her to confirm who I was talking about. "He and I broke up. Just recently got back together. There's magic here."

"That's what I'm hoping." Felicity smiled. Her face softened.

"I swear, that foster brother of yours..." Abby had made her way around the back of the bungalow and climbed the steps up to the deck. "This view of yours!" She gasped. "I miss him living here."

"But you have that fancy new house." I reminded her of how much she had wanted to be in a subdivision when I'd offered them the bungalow for as long as they wanted.

"I know. Don't remind me. Bobby Ray reminds me all the time that I'm spending money when I'm only spending it on things to make our house a home." Abby's voice held a little sadness before she focused on Felicity. "I'm sure you don't want to hear me whine when you're here for a vacation."

"More like trying to put my marriage back together," Felicity confessed. "The car was just a catalyst, something for him to use against me to say that he knew we shouldn't've come here. He'll throw that up in my face."

"Then we all need to go shopping for the perfect outfit for the Valentine's Day dance." Abby made a great suggestion.

"I love shopping." Felicity grinned.

"So do I," I confirmed even though I already had gotten the perfect Valentine's dance dress. But I supposed I could use a new one.

"Felicity?" Kirby interrupted our excitement of the shopping spree.

"Out on the deck," she called out to him.

"Why is the door open?" he asked her point-blank. "Do we have to pay for heat in this place?"

"Nope. All included. In fact, didn't Felicity tell you that your entire vacation is free because she won the Valentine's giveaway?" I asked and looked at Felicity so she'd play along. She gave me a questioning look, her brows furrowing before they finally sprung up high.

"No. She left that out." Kirby's head swung to look at Felicity.

"I was going to tell you as your Valentine's Day gift." Felicity went along with my impromptu story.

I was a sucker for love and couples getting back together.

CHAPTER 4

"No matter what you do, I don't think the Marshalls are going to make it," Abby whispered. She glanced over the romantic table we'd scored at the Red Barn that night.

"We can try." The conversation was between me and Abby since Felicity had excused herself to go to the bathroom.

Hank, Bobby Ray, and Kirby were discussing what was wrong with Kirby's engine. It was shoptalk that I didn't understand, but I certainly understood the look on Kirby's face.

He was mad.

"I reckon you've got me by the—" Kirby's finished sentence was a little colorful for my tastes, so I looked away to take in the band.

"Is that Corie?" Abby squealed and pointed to the dance floor at the front of the restaurant.

My eyes squinted through the dim lighting.

"I think it is." I took my napkin from my lap and put it on top of the table. "Let's go watch," I suggested, as it looked like a scene from one of those dance-competition television shows.

There were six couples in total. The men had on black

stretchy-type pants along with tight black button-up shirts and black shoes. I recognized a couple of the women as those walking out of the motel restaurant this morning when I was talking to Corie.

All the women had on the same black dress with slits to high heaven and tassels twisting and hitting their upper thighs with each turn. It had to have been planned. They were also all doing the same dance.

Every few seconds, you could see something fly out of the hands of the men and land on the ground.

"What is that?" Abby asked, pointing to the clumps of stuff.

"It looks like sawdust." I'd seen plenty of that stuff when I'd taken on the DIY project of redoing my old 1960s campervan.

Corie and Ricky had made it around the circle twice before she noticed me and Abby standing there.

"Abby and Mae!" Corie's eyes lit up when she saw us, then on her twirl, she saw Felicity. "Felicity!" she squealed right before Ricky held her arm above her head, twirling her so fast she looked like a black streak.

Abby and I moved over a little to let Felicity in the front with us. Ricky stopped twirling Corie as fast as he'd started and stood right in front of us.

"Felicity, may I have the honor?" Ricky had very good manners. He held out his hand, with his eyes fixed on Felicity.

She took his hand with a shy grin on her face, looking away slightly.

"Keep your eyes on your partner," Corie instructed right before Ricky literally swept Felicity up in his arms.

"Whoa, he's good," Abby gushed and clapped after Ricky dipped Felicity. There was nothing in the world that was going to wipe the huge smile off Felicity's face.

"She's not so bad either." I couldn't help but watch Felicity's head fall back, the bottom of her hair hitting the dance floor. Her smile was so bright, it light up Ricky's face.

Felicity's giggles could be heard across the restaurant when he jerked her back up into an upright position that lead them into another spin around the dance floor.

"See—right chemistry, right partner." Corie's brows lifted along with the edges of her lips.

The three of us broke out in applause once the song ended, but the commotion behind us overshadowed Felicity and Ricky's performance.

"I'm not going to let you take me to the cleaners just because I'm stuck here!" Kirby stood over Bobby Ray, who was sitting in his chair.

Kirby's arms were stiff next to his sides. His fingers closed then opened a few times before I noticed them really starting to form into fists.

"What's going on?" Felicity asked, pushing past me. She headed over to see what Kirby was talking about, her eyes scanning above all the onlookers.

Ricky followed her.

"Oh no." Abby's voice held dread.

It was like we could see what was going to happen.

"And you." Kirby pointed at Ricky. "You keep your hands off my wife."

Abby and I stood behind Ricky.

"If you knew how to handle your woman, you wouldn't be having these problems." Ricky squatted just in time to miss getting punched by Kirby, but Abby wasn't so lucky.

"Abby!" I screamed and bent down next to her but was flung onto the ground when Bobby Ray's hand landed on Kirby's jaw, causing Kirby to land on me.

"Get off me!" I tried hard to push Kirby off of me, but he was too heavy in his unconscious state, having been knocked out.

Then shrill screams coursed through my ears. My lungs struggled to get air. I gasped a full breath as Kirby was lifted from me. The bartenders and staff of the Red Barn were dragging people off of each other, some of them holding the trusty old baseball bats they kept behind the bar for rowdy times like these. Luckily, it seemed like the bouncers were able calm the crowd without using force.

"Mae." Hank's desperate look in his eyes turned to relief once he pulled me into his arms. "Oh god." He nuzzled me close amid all the commotion of people being cleared away from the area by the staff of the Red Barn.

"I'm fine," I assured him. "Is Abby okay?" I pushed away from Hank to find her.

She was sitting upright, working her jaw right to left. Nothing appeared to be broken, but I could hear Bobby Ray insisting she get checked out.

Sirens could be heard from a distance, which told me someone had called the sheriff, and not too long after it registered they were on their way, lights flashed through the Red Barn windows.

"I'm sorry, baby." Kirby's voice was desperate as he pleaded with Felicity. He sounded a bit weak and unsteady on his feet.

I sure hoped he wasn't suffering any concussion form being knocked out.

"I just couldn't take someone having their hands on you like that. And you were smiling, looking at him like you used to do to me."

"You've ruined my vacation here!" Felicity screamed at the top of her lungs. "Just like you do everywhere we go!"

"Baby!" He grabbed her by the arm when she tried to walk away. The sweet-talking was exactly like his pleas at the motel to get her back in Henry's car.

"Take your hand off her," Bobby Ray warned. "Or I'll take you down right here."

"Hold it right there, Bobby Ray," I heard Sheriff Al Hemmer's voice carry from above me. "We are going to take this down to the department and sort it all out." He snapped his fingers, and in no time, a couple of Daniel Boone Forest rangers appeared taking hold of Bobby Ray, Ricky, and Kirby.

"Kirby!" There was a fear in Felicity's eyes and voice as she called for her husband. "Please don't take him," she pleaded with Al.

"It's okay." I'd gotten up to go over to her. Not that it was my responsibility, but for some reason, I felt like she needed me since she was a guest of Happy Trails.

My phone chirped a text from my pocket. I ignored it.

"Let Al take them down to sort it out, and we will go pick them up. They all just need to cool down a little," Hank told her. "Al will let them go once they've let their egos deflate."

"Listen to Hank," I told her. "He used to be the sheriff, so he has firsthand knowledge."

Corie and Ricky's whispering caught my attention while Al continued to talk to a fiery Bobby Ray.

One of the rangers showed Ricky out of the restaurant, and Corie turned her attention toward me.

"Are you okay, love?" she asked.

"I'm fine. What about Ricky?" I asked.

"His ego is a little bruised, but he will be fine. I just hope this doesn't get out, or we will not be able to compete," she said, gnawing on her bottom lip.

"Will your friends say anything?" I asked, gesturing my chin toward the other five couples who had been dancing with them.

"No, but word has a tendency to go around." My phone chirped again just as the words left Corie's mouth.

"No joke." I laughed and pulled the phone from my pocket. It was a text from Betts.

She'd heard from Queenie's police scanner that there was a fight at the Red Barn Restaurant, and she knew I was down there.

Meet me at the campground if you're not busy, I texted.

I looked out at the darkness outside the window, knowing in reality it was around seven p.m. even though it appeared to be much later.

Stop by the Cookie Crumble. We needed some carbs and sugar.

CHAPTER 5

The night fell over the Daniel Boone National Forest like a blanket. I was silent while Hank drove us back to the campground, and I took in the shadows that poured down the forest trees, catching on cliffs and boulders before settling into the deep ravines and gullies the forest had to offer.

The silhouette of the trees reminded me of cloud formations, and I could almost see the outline of a dog's profile—the snout, pointy ears, and long neck.

I smiled.

"What are you smiling about?" Hank asked just as he pulled into the entrance of the campground. His hand felt across the seat and landed on my leg. He held the steering wheel with his other hand and kept it steady up the gravel road that led to the actual camping area.

"The scenery. It's so peaceful out there. Honestly, I need to keep out of everyone's business." I shook my head and got out of the truck once he put it in park.

The campground was cloaked in a stately quiet. But if I

listened closely, I'd be able to hear the creak of the late winter, the nighttime breeze as it flitted through the trees.

Hank let me sit with my comment as he pulled off to park his truck next to his camper.

The click and crack of twigs beyond the wooded tree line behind my camper let me know the nighttime animals were awake for the evening. The cicadas buzzed beneath the owl's hoot as the stars gradually started to show themselves off. This was how I knew it was going to be a gorgeous day tomorrow.

If the stars weren't visible, it meant the next day would bring rain.

I unlocked my campervan door and greeted Fifi. Her bowl of kibble was half eaten.

"Let's get our leash on," I told her and stepped up into the camper so she didn't bolt out on me before I could clip the leash on her collar. I put my purse down and looked at my phone to read the text thread with the Laundry Club Ladies, where they'd responded. I smiled, knowing they'd be here at any moment with some delicious cookies and an ear to listen about the night's events.

"Let's go get that fire started," I told Fifi and took her leash from the basket I kept right next to the captain's chair, which was placed for seating in my campervan. The basket was for Fifi's things, like her toys, her many sweaters, and a leash or two that I was too lazy to hang on the hook where they should've been.

There was no need to lock the camper door since I was going to be right back and it was safe here. By the time I'd gotten Fifi on her leash and out the door, the moon had come out from behind some lingering clouds. It hung over the lake, slivered like a slice of apple with a misty halo around it.

The naked ear would never know the road was a few hundred

feet away, carrying cars, trucks, and campers traveling at all hours of the night. Happy Trails Campground was tucked away from the hubbub of life and nestled between the mountains, which made me wonder what exactly was going on in Kirby and Felicity's marriage that this magical atmosphere didn't help solve.

"What on earth was going on?" Dottie asked. She'd beaten me to the communal firepit, located at the entrance of the campground just beyond the recreational center and next to the lake.

Henry was also there. He'd gotten the fire rolling, red and orange flames dancing between each other. There was a small stack of perfectly cut wood next to the pit for us to use up. Henry knew that when the Laundry Club Ladies got together, it could take all night. On a chilly night like tonight, we were going to need a lot of firewood.

"I don't know," I said flatly. "I honestly don't know."

I sat down in one of the Adirondack chairs, pulling a blanket off the back. After I curled my legs up under me and got Fifi in my lap, I pulled the blanket around my legs and over Fifi. She loved to sleep underneath blankets.

Instead of telling Dottie what I did know, I waited for the headlights to pop up from the very front of the campground and expose me and Dottie in their spotlight.

"I'll tell you everything I know once they get over here," I said and sighed. "I think we are going to have to put the Marshalls on the red list."

"Really?" Dottie questioned very excitedly, which told me she couldn't wait until she heard the details of the argument that'd taken place at the restaurant.

Betts and Queenie got out of Betts's cleaning van.

"I've got treats," Betts trilled through the darkness. She lifted her hand, and from the sound of it, she was shaking something, which ended up being a Cookie Crumble bag. "Christina was still there, and she made some fresh Valentine's cookies. She's not selling them at the bakery—she's making them for the special dance competition."

"If there's going to be one," I mumbled, hating to be the bearer of bad news.

"Do tell." Betts opened the bag and put it in my face for me to look into. "Don't spare any details."

"Wait. Where is Abby?" Queenie asked. She sat on the rock wall with her back to the fire. Her silver leggings were twinkling more than the stars that had started to make their appearance.

"I'm thinking she is at the sheriff's department, picking up Bobby Ray," I told them before I bit down into the delicious sugar cookie shaped like a heart.

I snorted and looked at the cookie.

"Much like this broken cookie," I said, holding it up, "I think there's more broken hearts this year during this Valentine's week than happiness."

"With Abby and Bobby Ray?" Betts asked and moved away from me to offer Dottie and Queenie a cookie before she got one and sat down next to me. "Henry! I've got cookies!" she hollered at him when he drove past us.

His golf cart skidded to an abrupt stop, and Henry jumped out.

"Thank you, Betts. That's mighty nice of you," he said with a smile and great big eyes as his hand reached into the bag to pull out a heart-shaped cookie with purple icing. "Mmm-mmm. I love me a good sugar cookie. And you know Christina makes the best. If you ladies will excuse me, I'll go see if the hot chocolate is ready."

"Hot chocolate?" Betts smiled and turned back to me. "I love hot chocolate. Anyway, what's going on with Abby and Bobby Ray arguing?"

"Yeah. I've never seen Bobby Ray and Abby argue like that. Of course they bickered a little when they dated, but I've never seen them actually have words. Bobby Ray had mentioned she was spending too much money," I noted. "I'm not sure what that meant."

"Abby did ask me if I would have a Tupperware party." Betts mentioned Abby's side hustle. "I haven't been to a Tupperware party or even had one since Abby started to sell them out of the office at the library."

"She asked if we used them in the recreational center for leftovers," Dottie said, her lips glowing from behind the lighter she'd flicked to light the cigarette sticking out from between them. She snickered. "I said, 'Leftovers? What leftovers?' These people don't leave leftovers if it's on our dime." She wagged her fingers while holding her cigarette, leaving a trail of smoke between us. "They will eat it all up and not leave a crumb. But they will haul out of here with all their coolers full."

"Well, we are their hosts," I reminded her.

"Back to Abby," Queenie said, pivoting back to the original topic. "What do you think is going on? Are they having financial problems?"

"I don't know. I guess I could ask Mary Elizabeth," I suggested. "Bobby Ray tells her everything."

"I thought he told you everything?" Betts asked and stood up from her chair to help Henry as he pulled up in the golf cart with the thermos of hot chocolate and stack of cups.

"He did tell me everything until he started dating our best friend." After Bobby Ray and Abby began dating, we grew farther apart on the more personal conversations. "He certainly doesn't tell me about his financial situation now that they are married."

It was true that Bobby Ray had needed a job when he moved to Normal. He'd also needed a place to live. I provided him with both, but it was truly his amazing skills as a mechanic that kept him on the job. He stayed, for free, in the bungalow the Marshalls were staying in. It was the only single-bedroom bungalow, and it was perfect for him. The other bungalows, lined up next to each other, were bigger. Some had a couple of bedrooms, while the biggest had four.

They weren't huge—they were cabin-style dwellings for people who wanted to visit the Daniel Boone National Park while enjoying the luxuries of a home. They were equipped with kitchens and bathrooms. They'd recently gotten heat and air-conditioning, so now I was able to rent them during the winter months, which I'd not done up until last year.

That was a big accomplishment.

When I'd inherited the run-down campground, the lake wasn't even fit for a frog to live, much less for people to swim, fish, or even ice skate during the winter months. The bungalows were mildewy and stinky. Plus, all the campers were neglected. Most of them had busted pipes where they'd never been winterized over the years, so I'd done a lot of work to get the campground even presentable enough to rent out a few.

And the three ladies sitting with me tonight around the fire were such a big help.

"We aren't going to solve that issue tonight. All we can do is support her, so one of us needs to have a Tupperware party," Betts suggested—a good idea.

We all nodded and took a cup of hot chocolate from her.

"Get to the good stuff," Dottie moaned. "The fightin'."

"It was really a great dinner out. The band was amazing," I told them.

"I heard it was the band they were using for the dance competition." Queenie's voice rose from the excitement of the competition she'd been so excited about. "A lot of my students and I ended up volunteering for the competition."

"If there's going to be one," I noted. Everyone looked at me.

"There still might be, but Corie and Ricky might not be competing."

"Why the heck not?" Dottie snarled, smoke rolling out of her mouth with each word.

"It was Ricky and Kirby who got into a fight"—I shook my head—"and then Kirby and Bobby Ray, after Kirby threw a punch at Ricky because Ricky told Kirby he didn't know how to keep his wife satisfied. Only, Ricky moved out of the way before Kirby made contact. That's when Abby was hit with Kirby's fist because she was standing behind Ricky."

The ladies gasped.

"Is she okay?" Betts cried out.

"So Bobby Ray clobbered 'im?" Dottie laughed and made the old one-two-punch gesture with her fists.

"That was one reason Bobby Ray felt it was appropriate to punch Kirby. Kirby had also been on Bobby Ray about the quote Bobby Ray gave them on their broken-down car." I gulped as images of how Bobby Ray was looking at Kirby when they were discussing the car floated into my mind. I didn't bother telling them the little details. "Even before the fistfight, things were brewing."

"How so?" Queenie asked.

"They were discussing the car, and that's when I suggested that Abby, Felicity, and I go up front and watch Corie along with the other dancers on the dance floor. I just wanted to get away from any arguments since Felicity was already on edge about what happened at the dance lesson."

"Huh. Some dance lesson." Dottie rolled her eyes. "If I had any money ridin' on this, I'd say that Corie loves to create controversy. Y'all know how some people just like conflict?" she asked but didn't bother giving any space for us to answer.

In fact, she didn't want us to answer.

"She's that type." Dottie leaned back, crossing her arms. "She tried to tell me and Henry that we had chemistry. Me and that thing." Dottie's lips contorted as she threw a finger at Henry.

"Why you all riled up 'bout that?" Henry butted in. "I'm a catch."

"Catch and release after they figure you out, maybe," Dottie said in a sarcastic tone.

"And you think you're the cat's meow? The cow's milk?" Henry asked her.

"Seriously, are these two really fighting about this?" Betts asked as Henry and Dottie carried on in the background.

"You should've seen their faces when Corie even mentioned Henry take the dance lessons," I told her. "You two, we don't have to worry about that. We aren't asking you to be dance partners."

"I think he liked her saying that," Dottie chirped.

"I loved it, because it got underneath your skin, Dottie Swaggert." Henry laughed. "Not too many people can do that."

Betts, Queenie, and I stayed silent. Our eyes grew as we watched Dottie shift from side to side. Her eyes rolled upwards then sideways, then down like she was trying to brainstorm a comeback for Henry. I thought Dottie was going to have some sort of outburst by the way her mouth would open a few times before it snapped shut, but she didn't.

"Are you at a loss for words?" I asked, needing to confirm what I was seeing in the darkness.

"Look." Queenie popped up. Her face was illuminated by the warm glow of headlights. "I think it's Bobby Ray."

"It is," I noted and then got to my feet. Fifi didn't move. "Do you think he's got Abby?"

In fact, all of us stood up in anticipation.

Who he had was far from Abby.

The passenger door flung open, and out jumped Felicity and Kirby.

"I swear, you will pay for this!" Kirby yelled at Bobby Ray before he slammed the door and kicked the truck's tire.

"Stop it!" Felicity screamed back at him.

"Whatever!" Kirby shrugged her off. "You go on and hang out with dancer boy. You two seemed awfully cozy."

Kirby was doing double-time down the road to get to the bungalow, leaving Felicity behind.

"I don't know why I even try to make this marriage work, Kirby! You are impossible!" Her words bounced off the dark mountains. "You deserve whatever is coming to you!"

"There ain't no amount of good clean forest air that's gonna save them two." Dottie's words hung on the cold breeze as it swept past her and landed on the back of my neck.

CHAPTER 6

Dottie and I had tried so hard over the years to make Happy Trails Campground more than just a campground. It was an experience. One the guests wouldn't forget.

Unlike most campgrounds in the Daniel Boone Forest or the national park area, we offered hookups for all sizes of campers, not like the snobby campgrounds that only allowed the popular silver campers.

Yes. Even campgrounds could be snobby.

Not us. I even offered tent sites and bungalows. The spring season was upon us, and that meant a lot of our water activities would be also opening up. Two of those were kayaking and white water rafting down by the stream off one of the many trails that started in the woods of Happy Trails.

I was lucky Dottie was here when I took over and she was on board with making Happy Trails the best experience. We'd worked hard on cleaning the lake in the middle of the campground so we could offer swimming and paddle boating, as well as the beach and dock area for guests to lounge at.

Then we had the recreational room with games, a couple

laundry machines, bathrooms, shower rooms, and vending machines. The tiki bar between the recreational room and the lake was a guest favorite, especially during parties.

I was very excited about the Valentine's Day party we were hosting, and from the looks of it, Henry was too. He'd already gotten all the boxes from storage units on our property that were labeled with a big heart—Dottie's doing—and they were stacked on the ground next to the tiki hut.

"Good morning, Henry," I greeted him on my way around the lake while I took Fifi for her morning walk. "I love how you hung the hearts from the tiki hut ceiling."

"Thanks, Mae." He giggled and blushed. "I reckon everyone gets a little gushy this time of the year." He reached down and patted Fifi, satisfying her enough to take off into the woods to get a sniff of which creatures had visited last night while we were sleeping.

He got back up on his ladder to hang some more of the hearts he had laid on the top rung.

"Have you seen the Marshalls this morning?" I asked. "When I passed by their bungalow, it looked pretty peaceful, considering last night."

After Kirby had stormed off, Felicity joined me and the Laundry Club Ladies. She'd said Kirby was torn up about the car quote Bobby Ray had given them to fix whatever was wrong with it. When Kirby had told Bobby Ray to forget it, Bobby Ray told Kirby it was already taken apart and up on the car jacks at Grassel's Garage, where he worked.

From what Felicity said, Bobby Ray and Kirby made peace at the sheriff's department, where Kirby accepted a ride back to Happy Trails, but once they were in Bobby Ray's truck, all hell had broken loose, and the two men were back at it.

Somehow in there, Kirby had blamed Felicity for them being at Happy Trails and for the car breaking down.

The Laundry Club Ladies and I sat there, listening to her, but never offered any advice. I kept my invitation open for her to join me this morning on my hike.

"Yeah, I have," Henry said, his muscles tightening in his jaw. He continued hanging a few hearts. "I think they'll be packing up to go home today."

"What's going on with them?" I asked and searched through the box of decorations he'd put on the counter of the tiki hut so I could pass him a few more hearts to hang while he was up on the ladder.

"I took him down to Grassel's this morning. It was early, but he insisted he wanted to be there first thing when Joel got there. I told him it was a late day for the garage to open, but he didn't care," Henry said and took the heart I was holding up. "I offered to get him a coffee from Trails Coffee, but he said he didn't want anything but to get his car and get out of this town, with or without Felicity."

My brows pinched.

"Good morning!" Dottie called from the open office window. Her nighttime hair cap was tugged all the way down to her forehead and over her ears. "I've got Fifi. She was scratchin' at the door. You headin' out?"

"She's in a mood today." Henry snorted and continued to decorate.

"I'll talk to you later," I told him and walked toward the office. "I am. I've got that new trailhead to check out. If it's as good and clean as reported to the committee, I think they'll be able to get it open before summer."

"Oh, goody." Dottie's eyes betrayed a tightness that told me she wasn't all that pleased. She pulled the hair cap off her head and started to unclip the hot-pink foam rollers from her red hair. "Another trail for more congestion. This place already has more people than ants."

I laughed. "You and I live on those people," I told her through the window. "And from what Henry said, we might have a bungalow open by the end of the day." She knew exactly who I was talking about. Her eyes grazed my shoulder as she looked toward the far end of the campground, where the bungalows were located.

"Me and Fifi will start going down the list." She ran her hands through the curls all over her head, letting them slide through her fingers and become a little more relaxed.

"I'm going to go see if Felicity still wants to go this morning." I said my goodbyes and turned to head back toward the Marshalls' bungalow.

I had gotten appointed to the National Park Committee and many other organizations after I'd showed the town folks just how good I was at bringing business back to the economy after Normal had seen a decline in tourism. They loved how I incorporated the local businesses into campground activities to promote them and how I upgraded the campsite so tourists would love staying and do more activities not only at Happy Trails but at the surrounding campgrounds.

I'd even gotten a key to the city, which wasn't an actual key but a plaque with a big gold key glued on it over my name. That motivated me to teach a business class to the local high school students, which then led to me getting appointed to the board.

It wasn't a huge job, but one of my responsibilities was to check out inquiries for possible new trails in and around the Daniel Boone National Park. Most of these were found by rangers who were called out to find lost hikers who had thought they were going down a marked trail but in reality had taken a deer trail or some sort of trail creatures in the night made. Legitimate trails had signs the general hiker or leisure walker wouldn't necessarily know to look for.

There were very few trailheads, or beginnings of trails, in the downtown area. So when Gert Hobson, the owner of Trails Coffee, had overheard a group of hikers talking about how they took a trail to the coffee shop, she reported it, since there wasn't a marked trail by that area. The committee had handed me the report, so I would now take my morning off, grab a coffee from Gert, and enjoy a nice early hike, which just so happened to be my favorite kind.

On my way back to see if Felicity wanted to go with me, I looked for Henry because I wanted to follow up about what had happened with Kirby once they arrived at the gas station, but he wasn't around, as far as I could see. Instead of searching for him further, I decided that if Felicity was going to go with me, she might tell me what was going on.

"Hi there." I greeted Felicity with a smile when she opened the door. The dark bags under her eyes and frazzled look on her face told me she'd not slept the greatest.

"Mae, I..." She frowned. "Do you want to come in? It's your bungalow."

"No, thank you. I am actually here to see if you want to go on that hike with me. Remember?" I was met with her head bobbing up and down, her mouth slowly closing before the corners of her lips turned up slightly.

"I'm sorry. You did invite me, and I already forgot." She rolled her eyes and laughed. "I'm not usually like this."

"You don't need to say anything to me. I just wanted to make sure you knew you could come with me to get some exercise and fresh air." I leaned in and said out the side of my mouth, "There might just be a big cup of coffee and tasty treat from Trails Coffee in store too."

"How can I refuse? Let me get ready."

"No problem. I have to go back to my camper and grab some items for marking something on the trail. So when you're ready, walk up to my camper, and we will hop in my little car," I told her, and she agreed.

I didn't tell her Grassel's Garage was also right in the downtown area because I didn't even want to go by there. If Bobby Ray was there—and that was a big *if* because Grassel's didn't open this early—I didn't want to see or hear another fight. Nor did I want to get swept up into anything with the sheriff's department.

"I'm sorry about last night," Felicity said once we'd arrived in town after a very quiet ride. We parked next to the Laundry Club, the laundromat Betts owned. The parking lot was open for public parking, and I didn't want to take up any spots on either side of the one-way streets downtown. Those were for tourists, and besides, the walk would do Felicity some good.

"You don't have to apologize to me," I said and led the way across the street to the grassy median that divided the main street into one-way streets. My backpack was strapped over one shoulder, and Felicity helped me position the other strap when she noticed I was struggling to get it over my arm.

"This is an adorable area," she noted, referring to the huge oak trees that made it look like a big park had been plopped down in the center of a road. She'd brought a walking stick with her from the campground, which she said she used for hiking around Happy Trails, and used the stick to help her along the street.

"We do a lot of festivals here. The amphitheater"—I pointed to the far end—"is really fun during the summer when the local theater puts on plays. We also have a big Christmas festival here."

We passed by a couple of the picnic tables on our way through. "Tourists and hikers love to come here and picnic. As you can see, all the shops are converted old houses from when this used to be a mining town." I gave her a quick history on how people would travel through, find something they could make money off of, and settle here for a few years before they moved on. "This was the area where they all lived, and the Historical Society has made sure they keep their shops as close to the original form as possible, even down to the side courtyards."

Every shop still had a side courtyard with a picket fence around it. The shop owners had come up with a lot of creative ways to use those throughout the years and seasons. Gert Hobson always made the Trails Coffee courtyard a little outdoor café adorned with twinkly lights.

"Good morning!" Gert called out. I stepped into the whiz of blenders and percolating coffee, and the smells wrapped around me. "I'm excited to see what you find out this morning."

"Me too." I headed on back to talk to Gert, leaving Felicity to look at the living wall Gert had had a special architect design. It was comprised of real plants and flowers indigenous to the Daniel Boone National Forest. She had paid really good money and still paid for its upkeep, the addition of seasonal flowers.

"This is amazing," Felicity said and laid her hand over her heart.

"Gert, this is Felicity." I began the introductions. "She and her husband are guests of Happy Trails celebrating their five-year anniversary."

"We aren't married," Felicity said, stopping me in my tracks. I had made the reservation when her name made it to the top of the wait list. We'd had a full conversation about their five-year.

"I mean, not legally, but in all senses of the institution, we are." She desperately wanted to clarify.

"Most people aren't nowadays." Gert offered a tight smile before she looked at me. "I've got a thermos for you to take if you want to. It's pretty compact and will hang off your loop."

Gert picked up a thin thermos with a red-and-black buffalo check pattern. It was the old-school kind with the twist-off lid that could be used as a cup. "I don't have two or an extra cup, but you could share." Gert shrugged as she came up with her best solution.

"I think we are just going to get two coffees to go and possibly a treat." My eyes scanned down the glass display case that contained some homemade treats. "Felicity, what would you like?"

"I think I'll just have a cinnamon bagel," she said, her fingernail clicking against the glass.

"Me too." I wanted to make it easy.

"I'll have it ready in a second." Gert plucked a piece of parchment paper from its holder and made her way down the case.

I took some steps away from the counter and stood next to Felicity so the next customer in line could get waited on.

"I love how she made tables out of the bourbon barrels." Felicity started to point out all the little details Gert had used to incorporate what Kentucky was all about. "Even the barrel-lid lazy Susans are adorable."

Gert had taken the lids of the bourbon barrels and repurposed them into lazy Susans that sat in the center of the tables and held all the condiments. It was a truly neat idea and worked so well.

"Mae!" Gert called after a few minutes and gestured to the opposite side of the counter, where the pick-up orders were placed when they were ready. "Be sure to stop in and let me know what you find."

"Will do," I told her on our way out the door. We walked past a few of the shops and turned into the alley that would take us behind the houses, where the hikers said the trail ended.

I explained to Felicity what I was doing and how the trail might be rocky at times or how we might end up having to turn around if it didn't look certifiable as a trail. "I'm boring you," I realized after we'd gotten to the beaten-down grass. I'd been talking Felicity's ear off about the process and paperwork it took to get a trail approved.

I stopped at the incline. I turned my body around to get a view from every angle and looked at my Daniel Boone National Park trail map to see where the closest marked trail was located.

"I think it's fascinating." Her smile was a little bit bigger and a lot more relaxed. "This is what I wanted me and Kirby to do. Go hiking. Leave it all behind."

The map crinkled in my hands as I manipulated it to face in the same direction we were.

"And I don't think I've seen a paper map in a long time." She laughed and took my cup of coffee when I held it toward her.

"I might be young, but it's got to be precise, and sometimes I don't get the trails as accurate with a GPS." Plus, everything still had to be stacked off, but I didn't want to bore her with the details. I took a small can of spray paint out of my backpack and started to lightly draw symbols on the ground so that whoever came out after my report could corroborate exactly what I was talking about in the documents.

"So, I was taken aback when you said you and Kirby aren't married, because I talked to you when you made the reservations." Not that I was calling her out, but I felt I deserved some sort of reasonable explanation.

I put the spray paint back in my backpack and took my coffee from Felicity so we could be on our way.

"Kirby doesn't believe in marriage, but he believes in monogamy. I've always taken him for his word and called it 'married' since I felt like we were going to be partners for life. I know I'm young and maybe naive, but I believe in love." She grinned. "Especially during Valentine's month."

"Do you want to get married?" I asked and took the flat grassy trail. I reached around with my free hand and grabbed the compass clipped onto my backpack. We were going west.

"Of course I do. Kirby makes it sound so romantic when he talks about how being life partners is more of a commitment than a marriage certificate, and when I reminded him of it last night, he stormed out of the bungalow." She got behind me as she spoke because the trail was getting thinner as we walked along.

"This is a deer path for sure." I pulled my phone out of my pocket and snapped a few photos before we proceeded farther. "See how the narrowing is really for a deer, and you can see some of their scat?" I pointed to the small round balls of waste dotting the trail.

"My goodness. This is really fascinating. Thank you," Felicity said and took her phone out. "Can I take photos?"

"Of the scat?" I thought that was odd.

"No, just of our walk." She let out a genuine laugh.

"Sure!" My voice escalated. I was happy to hear her joy.

There was a ruffling of leaves as something stirred in the forest.

"What was that?" Felicity's eyes grew, and she walked a little closer to me.

Out of the corner of my eye, I saw a white flash of a bushy tail low to the ground near a tree trunk.

"I bet it's a skunk," I told her and turned my back to her. "Unzip the front pocket and take out my little binoculars."

Felicity did exactly that and handed them to me.

"Just like I thought." I couldn't stop my big, fat smile from taking up my entire face. "It's a mama skunk and her babies." I handed her the binoculars.

"She's fairly big," Felicity whispered. "I didn't realize their noses were so long, and the stripe is literally running down the length of her body."

She was so excited. I let her ramble on and on about what she was seeing.

"Her tail is very elegant." She admired how gorgeous the mother skunk was in spite of the scent, which I was glad we hadn't smelled because the mother didn't feel we were a threat.

It was then that the skunk sprayed her victims.

"Her tail is literally trailing behind her like a feather boa." She pulled the binoculars from her eyes and looked at me. Her jaw had dropped.

"Did you know skunks live a long time, even in the forest? They don't spray unless they are threatened. Their predators learn their lesson pretty darn fast, which keeps the skunk very protected." I gave her a brief history on the skunk's survival skills. "They give birth in early spring, and she's probably teaching her babies to forage for berries and roots. They are very good gardeners and live pretty much solitary lifestyles. Happy little creatures."

"Maybe I need to be a skunk." She laughed.

"We could all be a little bit skunk." I snorted and looked down the hill through the barren trees that'd yet to grow their spring dressings.

She took a picture of a huge oak tree. Its root was so large it grew around a huge boulder. The oak looked as if it was tired and had rested itself on top, letting its weight down.

"Trees just grow everywhere here." I laid a flat palm on the trunk. "Doesn't it look like the tree is leaning on the big rock with its elbow?"

Felicity nodded as she moved around the large oak to take it all in. The mother skunk and her babies still didn't scurry off. They didn't seem to be bothered by us, though they still kept their distance.

"It does." She smiled and took more photos. "It's like the base of the tree is the thickest part when I assumed it would be the trunk."

"You can see how old these are." I pointed above us to show

her the natural archway the old trees had formed over top the trail we were checking out. "It's beautiful when the trees are dressed in their leaves."

I sucked in a deep breath and wondered what types of photos hikers would take if this were an approved trail. The spring and fall were really the most spectacular times, as Mother Nature loved to show off the national forest. It was a glorious sight no camera could even truly capture.

"Have you ever heard of the famous Kentucky bluegrass?" I asked her and made my way back over to the boulder and the large oak. "If you look down, below the boulder and between the tree's branches that form the little natural den around the rock, you'll see another rock formation."

I bent down and pointed to it as she hovered over me to see.

"I have heard Kentucky is called the Bluegrass State," she confirmed.

"That is because of that stone there, limestone." I gave her a brief history of limestone and the minerals and nutrients it provided for our horses, which made them big and strong.

"Did you hear that?" I stopped talking after I heard someone.

The mother skunk must've heard it too. There was a lot of scurrying going on, and a flash of black-and-white tail was the last thing I saw when I glanced back into the woods.

"Some yelling, maybe?" Felicity asked and swayed her body back and forth to see down the hill. "What is that down there?"

"That's the back of Grassel's Garage," I told her without even thinking.

"Kirby." She gasped and started to slide her way down the hill.

"Stop, Felicity!" I called after her and growled at myself for losing control of the situation. "I don't know if the terrain is stable, and you could break an ankle."

"I'll take my chances," she cried out without looking back.

"Why?" I asked myself and grabbed ahold of various tree trunks as I made my way down. "Why do I take on other people's problems?" Helping people had become a crutch for me over the last few years.

"Thank you, Alvin," I said to myself, because it was Alvin Deters from Deter's Feed-N-Seed who'd talked me into the expensive hiking boots with the tread that would guarantee to prevent me from sliding on my heinie all the way down the hill. "Felicity!"

I continued to yell, trying not to fall on my way down the rocky mountainside so I could keep an eye on her.

"Wait! Wait for me! I can talk to Bobby Ray." In my head, Bobby Ray was in the bay of the garage, putting the smack down on Kirby.

My feet finally planted on solid grass, loose rocks falling around me from the trail I had unearthed behind me. I glanced back at where I'd come from and shook my head, thinking I was lucky I didn't fall and break anything.

"Felicity?" I continued to call for her on my way around the garage building.

She was already inside the office space adjacent to the garage area where Joel Grassel and Bobby Ray worked with customers. It was just a glass enclosure with a fold-out chair and a long desk, and it smelled of oil, gas, and grease. There was a vending machine in the corner, but from what Bobby Ray had said, it didn't work unless you rocked it back and forth on its feet to jar loose what you'd keyed in to purchase.

"It doesn't look like anyone is here." Her eyes softened. "I guess I'm a little jumpy since our car is on the lift out there." My eyes looked to where she gestured, through the window in the office door that led to the garage.

"I don't mean to pry, but Henry told me he dropped Kirby

here off this morning." I walked up behind her and looked at their car.

There were parts strewn all over the floor underneath it. Though it looked a mess to me, I knew Bobby Ray had a system, and he knew where every single part went to make their vehicle work.

"I knew he'd gotten a lift but didn't know where. We had another argument. He said that he was going to go find Ricky and beat him up," she said with a hint of sadness. "I was hoping he was here."

"Come on, we can walk back on the sidewalk," I told her right before she opened the door leading into the garage.

"I'm going to grab my coat out of the back seat if you don't mind." She didn't wait for me to answer her, or I would have told her to forget her jacket since I had no idea how to lower the lift enough for her to get inside the car.

"The car is running!" She gasped and reached down to pick up a large metal remote control–looking thing with a red and a green button. She hit the red button, and the car started to descend.

I hurried over to the garage door, where I punched the garage-door opener to let some air into the garage because I knew carbon monoxide was poisonous.

"I can't believe Bobby Ray would keep a car running," I said to Felicity and turned back around to watch the tires of the car land on the cement floor of the garage.

"What?" she asked when she noticed the look on my face.

I licked my lips and said, "I think Kirby found Rick." My eyes fixed upon Rick's lifeless body in the back seat of Felicity's car. As if in slow motion, my eyes took in Felicity's hand dropping the metal remote control onto the garage's cement floor.

CHAPTER 7

"Where is Kirby now?" Al Hemmer asked Felicity. He had a wide-stance authoritative position going on with notebook in hand and pen at the ready to write down what Felicity had to say.

While Al was questioning her, I'd called Bobby Ray's and Abby's phones several times. I'd even left voicemails and text messages for them.

"I don't know. When Mae was calling you, I tried texting and calling him, but he's not answered." Felicity pushed her hair behind her ear with a trembling hand. "I don't think he did this."

"According to Mae, Henry Bryant dropped your husband off here this morning." Al was not yet privy to the fact that the Marshalls weren't married.

"He's not my husband," Felicity murmured. "We are life partners."

"Life partners?" Al asked with a flat voice, letting his hand to fall to his side. "What is that?"

"They are committed to each other like husband and wife," I told him.

"Whatever you are, I have a deputy heading over to the

campground to get a statement from Henry." Al pulled the notebook back up and started to write something down. "Not married."

"What does that have to do with anything?" Felicity asked.

"I reckon nothing, but it needs to be corrected from last night's file." Al glanced up. "After Bobby Ray dropped you and Kirby off, did Kirby say anything else about Rick?"

"No. He was so mad about how much the car was going to cost to be fixed that he was saying things about Bobby Ray." Felicity continued to check her phone. "Why aren't you questioning Bobby Ray? It's his shop."

"Don't you worry about who we are and aren't questioning." Al sucked in a deep breath. "I need to check on something. Don't move."

Felicity typed on her phone while I watched everything going on around me. One of those things was Al. By the way he was muttering to a deputy sheriff and seeing the deputy into his car, Al hadn't yet called on Bobby Ray but didn't want me or Felicity to know that.

There were a couple of rangers inside the garage and another deputy surveying the entire gas station. Al didn't come back over to us after the deputy drove off, in the direction of Abby and Bobby Ray's subdivision. Instead, he walked over to one of the gas pumps where Colonel Holz had parked the hearse.

Colonel Holz was our local coroner, and he'd be the one to assess Rick's body before they would move him. This was crucial to the case against any of Al's suspects. Colonel had told me once that the body always revealed what had happened. In the case of a murder, he believed that the corpse told you who killed them—you only had to listen to them.

It sounded creepy, but he knew what he was talking about.

The sound of screeching tires from Joel Grassel's truck

taking the turn into his gas station made me turn and watch Al hurry over to Joel, stopping Joel from running up to the office. With his hand on Joel's chest, Al appeared to have talked Joel down to a somewhat-calm state.

"I've got to talk to Colonel," I overheard Al tell Joel. "You are more than welcome to go over there and wait with Mae."

Joel shot me a look and lifted his chin in acknowledgment. It was a look I'd seen on him before, after his brother had passed away. It was a look that you never forgot.

I left Felicity there, though she didn't even notice, and met Joel halfway.

"What on earth is going on? I got a call from Agnes telling me someone was found dead at the garage. You're here." He ran his hand over his face. He let out a long sigh and looked at the garage again.

"I know. Here I am again," I grumbled. "Have you heard from Bobby Ray?" My gut tugged at me since I knew Al had sent a deputy Bobby Ray's way.

"I talked to him late last night. He called to tell me not to work on the car this morning because the owner wasn't happy with the estimate. I was planning on coming in and putting the parts back in, but I'm guessing the owner is in there." He pointed to the garage bay.

"No. It's one of the local dancers, who just so happened to get into a fight last night at the Red Barn with the owner of the car—" I tried not to place blame or point a finger at Kirby, but it was kind of hard not to. "Kirby Marshall."

The name rattled around in my head until it clicked.

"Felicity Marshall made the reservation on her credit card." My jaw dropped, and my eyes slid up Joel's face and met his eyes.

"What?" Joel's mouth contorted to one side.

"You just helped me with something. I've got to go talk to

Felicity." I put my hand on his forearm. "Let me know if you hear from Bobby Ray."

Colonel Holz and Al had gone into the garage bay. Colonel was walking around the car, and Al was getting an update from one of the rangers. By the shakes of their heads, it seemed they'd not gotten any more clues than those I knew.

"Anything?" I asked and looked at Felicity's phone.

"No. His phone keeps going to voicemail." She looked up at me with tearstained lashes. "Do you think he's okay?"

"I'm sure he is. But I have to ask you something." I didn't want to mislead her into thinking her partner wasn't a prime suspect. "You reserved the bungalow under your name and your credit card. If you and Kirby aren't married, what is his last name?"

"Barringer. Why?"

"I hate to even think this, but if Al thinks this is a murder…" I stopped to collect my thoughts. "I'm just wondering why this guy was in your car with the engine running."

"Who knows. Look around, Mae—your town isn't Normal like the name claims." Felicity teared up again. "Where is Kirby?"

"I've helped the Normal sheriff's department out on a few cases." I could see by her wide-eyed look that she was a smidgen confused. "I have a knack for finding things out, in particular about crimes." I waved my hand. "None of that matters. What matters is I'm good at it. My boyfriend, Hank"—I knew she knew him, but I wasn't sure how much she was able to comprehend in her state of mind—"he's a private investigator now, and I just can't help but think he might be able to help if we need him."

"What does this have to do with Kirby's name?" Felicity brought me back to my original question.

"I hate to even think it…" I hesitated because I was about to let her know exactly how Al Hemmer thought through these types of cases. "I've been around Al Hemmer for years, and I can almost see into his thought process on these things. I'm sure he's thinking Bobby Ray and Kirby had something to do with this."

"Kirby?" She gasped. "Not my Kirby. He's a lot of things, but a killer he is not."

"I feel the same about Bobby Ray, but it doesn't make the evidence go away." I sighed, realizing I was going to have to break this down. "I'm not a lawyer by any stretch of the imagination. I've watched a lot of crime shows, and I've seen a lot in the last few years to make me somewhat of an amateur when it comes to the real thing." I wanted to be very upfront with my lack of expertise and schooling in the field of crime. I took great pride in my logical side.

"I'll start with Bobby Ray." If I cleaned up what I considered my side of the street first, maybe she'd take what I had to say about Kirby a little better. "Kirby wasn't happy with the price Bobby Ray put on fixing the car."

"Because it was—is—highway robbery," she blurted out.

"I'm not sure what the price tag was, but I'll take your word for it." I also knew sometimes you had to use honey to make things a little sweeter, because I could tell she desperately wanted this to be Bobby Ray's doing and rightfully so. "Besides, we don't even know if this is a crime or not. Al will sort it all out."

I really wished I had as much confidence in Al as I was telling her.

"You're right. If this wasn't Rick's own doing, then someone did it." Felicity wiped her hand over her tearstained cheek.

"Al will look at Bobby Ray like he was trying to get back at Kirby for the public fight they had at the Red Barn. It seems ridiculous, but if word got out that Bobby Ray was charging too much, then business would die down or go away. If Bobby Ray's livelihood was in jeopardy, what man wouldn't stop it at the source?" I shrugged.

Oh no. The lines between my eyes pinched. What if I was right? I tucked what had come out of my mouth in the back of my head.

"Bobby Ray could've killed Ricky to frame Kirby so that Bobby Ray could tell people how Kirby was dishonest and a killer, making his business look good where Kirby made him look bad." Felicity suddenly had her thinking cap on.

"On the other hand..." I had to stop that thinking train in Felicity's head. "Kirby was mad at Bobby Ray. Kirby also heard Bobby Ray and Ricky have words at the dance lesson. Kirby did try to punch Ricky out. Kirby was dropped off here by Henry this morning. Now there's a dead body of the guy who they all were hauled down to jail for, and he's nowhere to be seen."

We glanced over at the gas pump, where Bobby Ray pulled in with Abby in the truck.

"Bobby Ray is here." I had to throw it in for the sake of driving my point home about Kirby. "Where's Kirby?"

"I don't know." She blinked a few times and went back to her phone. "Please answer," she pleaded into the mouthpiece after she put it up to her ear.

I slipped away to talk to Abby after Al made his way over to Bobby Ray.

"What is going on?" Abby's eyes were red, as though she'd been crying.

"You tell me." I wrapped my arm around her shoulder. "It looks like you know more than you want to tell me."

"No. I don't," she insisted. "Why was Ricky even here?"

"Last night?" It was merely a suggestion.

"If that's the case, I do know what it looks like, and you know I know," she whispered, "that Bobby Ray looks like he killed that dancer."

"Good news is Kirby Marshall—um, Barringer—" Abby gave me a confused look. "Those two aren't married, but I'll tell you about that later. Henry told me Kirby asked him for a ride here this morning. Ricky is dead, and Kirby isn't anywhere to be found."

"Then he did it." She threw her hands in up in the air. "Bobby Ray didn't. Besides, we were home all morning, fighting."

"I am so glad to hear that." When she looked at me with a dropped mouth, I clarified, "Not the fighting part but the part of him having an alibi."

"Honestly, Bobby Ray wouldn't kill anyone." Abby didn't tell me anything I already didn't know.

"We know that, but she doesn't." I pointed with my eyes at Felicity, who was still jabbing around on her phone.

"Abby." Al Hemmer interrupted us from afar and gestured for her to come there. I followed her when I noticed Felicity was heading his way too. "I'm gonna need you to tell me your whereabouts this morning."

"Her whereabouts? What about his?" Felicity interjected. "He's got the most to lose from this ordeal. He is framing Kirby because Kirby is exposing him for what he is—a robber! He's killed that man as a way to get Kirby in jail and silence him because Kirby is going to bring him and his awful business ethics down! Ask his own sister. She's the one who came up with his motive." She bounced on her toes. "Oh my. Did Kirby walk in while you were killing Rick? What did you do with my Kirby?" she screamed.

"Ma'am, we are all just trying to figure this out." Al tried to stop her. "No one even mentioned nothing 'bout killin' no one."

"You gave her a motive as to why I would do such a thing? Losing business? Geez, Mae." Bobby Ray gave me a hateful look.

"Really, Mae?" Abby's eyes blinked rapidly. "You just told me that Kirby was framing Bobby Ray because he was getting him back for the cost of the repairs and Ricky for hitting on Felicity."

"I-I..." I literally stammered over my own words before both women stormed off in opposite directions. "Bobby Ray, you can't possibly think—" I slammed my mouth shut when he stuck his hand up in my face.

"I don't know what to think," he snarled. "After everything I ever did for you."

"I didn't mean..." I was left standing there with both feet in my mouth.

CHAPTER 8

"Henry, are you there?" I asked and pulled my phone from my ear to see if we were connected.

"Yes. I'm listening," he said.

"I need you to tell me exactly what Kirby said to you this morning when he asked you to take him to the garage." I watched through the windshield of my car as Al walked into the sheriff's department with Bobby Ray, Abby, and Felicity following. I had to know if Al was going to hold either of them, and I was determined to help them even if I had to call on my friend Ava Cox.

"I was cutting some wood, and he asked me if I could give him a ride to town to get his car. I drove him there, and that was it."

"What did he talk about? Anything?" I asked.

"He mentioned something about fishing, and I told him how much I loved it, and I gave him a pole when we got back," he said.

"Got back?" I asked.

"Yeah. I told him the garage wouldn't be open and around here things are just slow and easy. When he saw no one was there, we came back and I gave him a fishing pole and had him go on down to the stream off Red Fox Trail." Henry had just given me Kirby's location.

"Have you talked to Al today?" I asked.

"Nope. Why?" Henry had yet to hear what had happened.

"There was a body at the garage, and I'm not sure if it's a homicide because it appears that carbon monoxide played a part, but there's no reason for Ricky to have been there." I turned the engine off so I could at least go inside and tell Al as well as Felicity where they could find Kirby. "Did you happen to see anything unusual?"

"Nope. Not a thing." Henry was a man of very few words. "I'll keep noodling it, but it was pretty straightforward talk about fishing."

"Thanks, Henry." I got out of my car to go into the department to let them know Kirby was fishing.

The sheriff's department was located in the back of the Normal Courthouse. The entrance was on the side, and as soon as you walked in, you had to see Agnes Swift to be buzzed in.

"Who are you?" I asked the young lady sitting in Agnes's chair.

She leaned up on Agnes's desk to slide the small window open.

"What did you say?" she asked me, shoving a piece of her long red hair over her shoulder.

"Where's Agnes?" I asked her.

"She's out. I'm here from the ranger's department to sit in for her while she's out," she said. "How can I help you?" She grabbed a rubber band off Agnes's desk. She gathered her hair in one hand and wrapped the rubber band around it, creating a bun at the nape of her neck.

"What's your name?" I asked.

"Pearl." She smiled. "It was my gram's name. I'm not nearly old as my name."

"I didn't think you were. I'm Mae, and Agnes is my boyfriend's granny. I didn't know she wasn't here today." I had to call Hank.

"She's sick. I reckon she's got the stomach bug. Throwing up out of both ends, if you know what I mean." Her nose curled.

My attention moved to behind Pearl. Al was talking to Bobby Ray and Abby before he showed them down the small hall that led to the interrogation rooms.

"I'm also here with Bobby Ray and Abby." I gestured behind her. "And Felicity." I said it loud enough to get Felicity's attention. "Kirby is at the campground!"

"He's what?" Felicity's voice rose. "Did you say the campground?" She shoved her way next to Pearl and shook the phone at me. "No wonder he's not answering my phone. He must've accidentally took mine because this one is his." Her forehead wrinkled. "I just can't believe he didn't see my pink phone cover."

Felicity had leaned on the dispatch desk.

"Um. Excuse me." Pearl leaned back and shot Felicity a look. "My space." She used her hands to make large circles around her. "Your space." She pointed to a chair.

"Can I please come inside to talk to her?" I asked Pearl.

Pearl gave an exhausted sigh before she got up off of Agnes's stool to let me in the door.

"Do you mind telling Al that the man they are looking for has been fishing this entire time at the campground?" I asked Pearl, receiving a flat look from her.

"Fine." Pearl left me there with Felicity.

"The good news is Kirby is fine. When Henry took him to the garage this morning and he realized the garage wasn't open—even though Henry told him," I muttered under my breath,

"Henry took him back to the campground and let Kirby borrow a pole to fish."

"I didn't think you allowed fishing in the lake," she said. Obviously, she'd read the signs we had posted.

"We don't, but did you see Red Fox Trail?" I asked then explained, "It's a trail up near the tiki hut. If you hike down about a mile, you will run into a large stream where warmer-weather activities are offered. You can fish there anytime." I smiled. "Isn't it great he's there?" I wanted to point her to the bright side of things.

"Yes. But that man—" A shadow cast down her face. "In the car—" She spoke in broken sentences. "They said he was murdered hours before that then put into the car as a cover-up. Hit over the head with something."

The good news I thought I'd had for her soured real fast.

My phone buzzed. I pulled it out of my pocket and answered when I saw Hank's name.

"Hi, Hank," I answered and stepped away from Felicity. "How is Granny Agnes?"

"I was calling to let you know about her. She's pretty sick to her stomach, and they've got her in the hospital down in Beattyville," he said. "They are going to give her some IV fluids and oxygen, but they think she's going to be okay."

The hospital in Beattyville wasn't big. It was more like an emergency room, and if you needed more care, they would transport you a couple of hours away to a bigger hospital in either Lexington or Louisville.

"She's going to be okay. It doesn't mean I'm not worried about her." He loved his granny so much.

I swear I could feel the depth of his sorrow. Agnes Swift was more than just his mama's mom—she had raised Hank. It would be hard seeing the spry older woman in the hospital, much less on oxygen, when she could run circles around me.

"What about Precious?" I asked about Agnes's fur baby she'd gotten from me after Fifi had puppies. "Do I need to go get her?"

"Actually, that's where I've been all day. I went to the hospital to see Granny, then I went to her house to get Precious. After that, I took the dog back to the campground. I saw Henry, and he told me what was going on. I'm guessing you're at the sheriff's department?" He knew me all too well.

"Yes. I just heard Ricky's death is looking more and more like a homicide," I said, but I could hear Hank shuffling with something on the other end.

"Mae, hold on. I've got a call coming in from Jerry." He clicked over to answer.

Jerry Truman had been the sheriff previous to Hank. He ended up leaving and opening his own private-investigation services. It took some time, but after badgering Hank to join him, Hank finally did.

"Jerry just said Corie Sadek has hired us to look into Ricky's death," he said. "I'm heading down to the office. Want to come?"

"Interesting," I muttered, thinking about how fast Corie had called in help from a private detective. "She's not letting the police handle it?"

"She said something about needing it solved quickly for the sake of the competition." He offered up her convenient excuse.

"Or for the sake of her not looking like a suspect." All those odd stares and jeers I'd seen between the other dancers and Corie started to play in my head.

The obvious suspect was Kirby. Not only did he have a public altercation with Ricky at the Red Barn but he'd also gotten into that little scuffle during our dance lesson.

"I have to run to Happy Trails really fast, then I'll be down there," I said.

There were two prime suspects in my head: Kirby Marshall

and Corie Sadek. Before I heard from Corie, I wanted to get my thoughts about Kirby straight.

After all, it was his car where we found Ricky. Was it a coincidence? No way did I believe that. Either Kirby put Ricky there, or someone was setting Kirby up.

Corie.

There was a lot riding on this competition for her—a championship. From what she'd said, it was a very important one at that.

Though I'd hate to think she did this to her dance partner, the tone of her voice during the dance-lesson fight she'd had with Ricky was one you'd never forget. One that held a punch. One that told you she was serious. One that had consequences.

What was more of a consequence than death?

CHAPTER 9

Felicity needed a ride back to the campground, and since she was my guest, I felt obligated to give it since her car was incapacitated, but I also wanted to see Kirby. Al Hemmer was looking for him, but I needed to get a jump on talking to him before Al got there. I was sure Pearl would tell Al exactly what I'd said to Felicity, since she listened to the entire conversation. I had limited time.

"Can I please talk to him first?" I asked Felicity on our way over since I knew how the law enforcement worked here. "I need to ask him a few questions before the sheriff comes to question him." She agreed.

"Do you think I need to call a lawyer?" she asked, her eyes clouded with sadness. "I never thought this trip would've turned out like this." She looked out the passenger's-side window the entire drive back to the campground.

"I'm sorry. I hate to even think that you do, but you might want to call someone while I talk to him," I suggested.

She didn't say anything, only gestured with a nod of her head and kept silent the rest of the ride back to Happy Trails.

Instead of parking at the office or at my campsite, I drove

Felicity around the lake to drop her off at the bungalow, then I parked my car next to my campervan. That way, I could get Fifi and take her for a walk down Red Fox Trail on my way to chat with Kirby.

Fifi was so happy to finally be getting out into the sun. I still kept a little coat on her to ward off the chill since she'd recently gotten groomed. She would dart ahead of me then stop briefly to see whether I was coming or she needed to veer off course and follow me. I took the long way around the lake in order to avoid going past the bungalows.

There was a knock on the office window from inside. Dottie was waving to me from behind the glass. I waved back. Within seconds, my phone was ringing. It was Dottie.

"What are you doing?" she asked.

"Henry said he dropped Kirby off here after no one was at the garage." I passed by the decorated tiki hut on my way to the tree line where the mouth of the Red Fox Trail began. "Either Kirby didn't know about the murder yet, or he committed the murder then came back to have someone take him to the garage just so he had a witness and alibi."

"Betts, Abby, and Queenie already called about the event tonight. Is it still on?" she asked.

"As far as I know." Everyone was looking forward to the main event—the dancing.

"If I had my druthers, I'd think we all still need to go and see what's going on." Dottie had a way of letting me know she wanted to snoop around with me and the Laundry Club Ladies.

The Laundry Club Ladies was an endearing term that not only Betts, Abby, Queenie, Dottie, and I used to refer to ourselves but, over the past few years, that the community used as well.

Talk—as in gossip—or even just people who needed some information came to us, since we had an uncanny knack of finding things out that led to the truth and had helped the sheriff solve mysteries, which led to putting the bad guys behind bars where they belonged.

Of course, you had those who said we were just a bunch of nosy old broads, but I liked to think of the Laundry Club Ladies as amateur sleuths.

"Maybe we can give you your druthers." I laughed and clicked my tongue a few times to get Fifi back on the trail leading down to the stream where I was hoping to find Kirby. "Let me know if you hear anything in the meantime. What I know is Kirby is down here fishing, and I wanted to pick his brain before Al did."

"I'll go grab the notebook." Dottie had a key to my campervan. She wanted to get the spiral-bound notebook where the Laundry Club Ladies kept all of the clues we'd found for each case we decided to look into—

Snoop into.

Her key was also very convenient when Dottie was in the office and Fifi needed to go out. Not that babysitting Fifi was part of her job. Dottie enjoyed having Fifi around, and Fifi loved her just as much.

"You know where it is—in the drawer in the kitchen," I told her and carefully stepped over a fallen tree that must've rolled onto the trail over the winter. I made a mental note to tell Henry so he could clear the path even though it wasn't technically on our property since it was part of the forest. Still, I had no intentions of someone tripping over it and hurting themselves.

"Goodbye." She clicked off the phone. I slipped mine back into my pocket and continued to take the trail pretty slowly since it was the first time I'd been on it since last fall. Winter hiking wasn't one of my favorite things to do. Luckily for me and the campground, hikers loved to take the trails in any weather, still providing good business during what some outdoor companies would consider down months.

Red Fox Trail was named due to the red fox population in this area. Years ago, from what I was told, they'd actually beaten down the path from the woods to the stream where they'd drink, making it a trail of their own. So we didn't disturb their natural habitat. We did maintain the trail and woods around it as they made it, only marking the trail for hikers.

Creatures in the forest were creatures of habit, like humans. They took the same paths, day in and day out, making their own little trails. It was only natural for us to use some of those for safe hiking while keeping the integrity of the forest intact.

"Fifi!" I called when I didn't see her but heard some crunching of branches that was too loud for a little poodle to make.

Even though I didn't see any red foxes during the day, I knew they were out at night. Fifi would make a tasty little snack, which is why I put her on her leash at night, but during the day, I was very vigilant.

She darted back onto the trail with her little tail down.

"What did you see out there?" I asked her and smiled, thankful she'd come back. "Stay with me."

She was so good at taking commands. I wasn't the one to take credit for that, since she'd been a trained pedigree poodle before I became her second owner.

Eventually, we hiked our way down to the banks of the large stream, where I saw Kirby fly-fishing. He stood out in the middle of the stream, wearing Henry's waders and a flannel jacket, pulling in the line before flicking it out and repeating a few times until he noticed I was there.

"I guess you're here to give me a lesson about love and all that mushy stuff." He didn't look at me when he talked. He kept his eye on the line.

"Nope." It dawned on me that he had no clue what was at Grassel's Garage when he'd had Henry take him down there. He certainly didn't act nervous or edgy, which was how I would act if I'd killed someone. "I'm here to ask you a few questions about Ricky."

I realized I had no idea what his last name was.

"That dancer?" He gave me a quick glance.

"Yeah. The sheriff and everyone have been looking for you," I told him and kept a close eye on Fifi.

She was known to dive into water and swim around. Even she knew it was too cold by the way she stood at the edge of the stream, her toenails barely touching the water's edge.

"Sheriff? Did that tippy-toe file a restraining order on me?" Kirby shook his head. "Felicity said he would. I don't know what to do. I've apologized to her for the fist, and you were there—you know I didn't throw a fist to her."

"Actually, Kirby"—I took another step closer—"I hate to be the one to tell you this, but Ricky was found in your car at the garage."

"Why was he in my car?" he asked and reeled in the line.

"He's dead." I watched for a reaction.

"Dead." A chilly shock rose on his face. "What happened?"

"Someone wanted him dead. He was murdered."

"Murdered?" He held the long pole up in the air, almost above his head, as he walked through the stream to meet me on the banks. "I guess he flirted with the wrong guy's girl."

"Did you hear what I said about your car?" I wasn't sure if he'd heard me over the rolling water of the stream.

"Why was he in my car?" he asked, stopping right in front of me, his feet still in the water.

"That's what the sheriff wants to know." I continued to watch his facial expressions. Nothing stood out to me other than a little shock.

"He thinks I did it?" His head cocked back. "I didn't. You can ask your handyman. We didn't even get out of the car. He told me about fishing, and that's when I borrowed his pole until the garage decided to open."

He walked out of the water and grabbed the fishing bag. It was Henry's.

"I'm going to need a ride to the sheriff's office." He headed toward the trail. "Do you think I did it? What about Felicity? Does she know?"

Ricky's murder was starting to process in his mind. Something I'd seen before, after the initial shock of hearing someone was murdered, settled into my thoughts.

"Maybe we should talk for a second before you head up that way." It was just a matter of time before Al showed up at the campground, and if my guest, Kirby, hadn't done it, then I needed to be armed and prepared regarding what to do for him. I felt it was an obligation to provide and keep my guests safe. If he was accused of murder—and by the way he was acting, he sure didn't seem to have done it—then I wanted to know all the details.

"Are you some sort of cop or something?" He shook his head. "I don't understand this town."

"I'm not, but Hank is a PI." I wasn't sure how deep in conversation Hank and Kirby had gotten in the brief moments they'd spoken over the last couple of days, including at the Red Barn last night, but I told him anyways. "Since you are a guest of mine, if you didn't have anything to do with Ricky's murder, I want to be here to help you. Answering a few questions will get me and Hank started."

Hank's occupation was a convenient way to get someone to talk. Maybe it was a little manipulative, but it was for good.

"I guess it won't hurt. What do you want to know that you

didn't see with your own eyes?" he asked with a snarky undertone.

"Felicity and I found him. In fact, we went to the garage and noticed the car's engine was on. That's when we lowered the car and saw him." I gulped, trying to clear the sight from my memory. "She said you had left during the night, and I wasn't sure where or how you went."

"I did leave. I got an Uber and went back to the restaurant to throw darts and drink." The branches of the trees in the woods creaked and moaned over his voice in the light spring breeze.

"Uber?" I asked, knowing I could get ahold of the driver to confirm. Easy enough. "Did you talk to anyone at the bar? Throw darts with anyone?"

"The bartender."

Again, easy enough to get an alibi if that was where he was at the time of the murder, which was what I needed to figure out from Colonel Holz's preliminary autopsy.

"It's good you got an Uber and were at the bar." I wanted to give him some relief and let him think he could trust me.

"Why would I kill him?" He shook his head and glanced up the trail to where Fifi was sniffing around the base of the trees.

"One motive is Felicity. You did swing to hit him and miss. You sure didn't miss when you killed him." I knew it was hard reasoning for him to swallow.

"I told you—I didn't do it!" His voice boomed. Birds quickly flew from the trees into the sky.

"I understand that. I also know Sheriff Hemmer, and that's what he's going to say to you." I needed him to know how to handle Al.

"What do you suggest I do?" he asked.

"Felicity is calling in a lawyer for when you go down to the station for questioning. Henry can take you down to the station, and I can check out your alibis, the Uber driver and the bartender." There was more than enough for a starting point. "Let's start there. I'm going to need the Uber driver's information."

"Yeah, sure." He put the pole and bag back on the ground and took his phone out from the bag. He fumbled with the passcode a couple of times. "I must've grabbed Felicity's phone." He scoffed. "Pink case."

I smiled and waited patiently for him to figure out the phone passcode.

After he got his Uber app up, he showed the screen to me. "Here you go. Barry."

I looked at it.

"Can I take a photo of it with my phone?" I asked.

"Yeah, if it's going to help me get out of this mess." He held the phone steady for me to take a snapshot of Barry's name, his hand a little too steady for someone who was a suspect in a murder investigation.

At least, a suspect in my book.

CHAPTER 10

Just as I'd thought, Sheriff Al Hemmer was waiting at Happy Trails Campground when Kirby and I made it to the top of the trail.

Kirby told his story to Al and even showed him the Uber that he'd taken back to the bar.

Al had his thumbs tucked inside of his utility belt with his fingers splayed apart, a piece of grass stuck in the corner of his mouth, a flat look on his face, and big mirrored sunglasses to shield his eyes.

His demeanor told me he wasn't buying what Kirby was selling.

Turned out I was right. Al put Kirby in the back of his sheriff's truck and flipped on his lights to take him down to the department.

"Were those lights necessary?" Dottie snapped open her cigarette case and tapped out a smoke.

"You know Al." I sighed, my head tilted to watch as the lights disappeared down the drive and out of sight. I turned to Dottie and said, "He always wants to seem bigger than he is."

"What now?" Her thumb rolled the flint wheel of her lighter, landing on the button to bring the flame to life. She sat down in one of the plastic chairs in front of the office and kicked it back, teetering on its two hind legs with its back resting against the brick.

"I'm going to go down to Trails Coffee. Hank called before I talked to Kirby and said Corie contacted them to look into Ricky's murder." My words caused Dottie to stop midpuff.

"Really?" Smoke accompanied Dottie's words.

"Yep." I bent down to pick up Fifi so I could take her back to my campervan before she darted off and I had to catch her.

"What about Kirby's alibi?" She sucked in a draw.

I took my free hand and eased her chair back down onto all fours. "You're going to break a bone if you keep doing that," I warned. "I'm not sure about Kirby, but I did take a picture of his Uber app, and I plan on giving the driver a call as well as heading down to the Red Barn to talk to the manager. I want to see who the bartender on call that night was."

"I can call down to the Red Barn while you go listen to what Corie has to say. Not that I'd believe a word out of her mouth." Dottie had already made an enemy out of Corie in her head, all due to the fact Corie said Henry and Dottie had chemistry.

I kept my mouth shut.

"I'll even write all this down in the notebook." Dottie took one last puff of her cigarette before she bent down and dragged it along the concrete to snuff it out. "Welp. I better get back to work."

I was about to tell her goodbye when some gravel pinged in the distance, a sure sign someone was driving up to the campground.

Two cars followed, one after the other. The first I recognized as Abby's then realized the second was Kirby and Felicity's.

"Well, well. I reckon Al released the car," Dottie noted.

"And it's fixed," I said before I walked up to greet Bobby Ray.

"Here." He didn't make eye contact. "I fixed their car for free after Al said it was no longer needed."

"That was so nice of you." I put my hand on his forearm. "Can we please talk?"

Abby tooted the horn. Both Bobby Ray and I looked at her. She motioned for him to come on.

"Not now. Abby told Coke she'd come to help decorate for tonight's dancing event." He shrugged me off. "Listen, you know I love you, but you hurt me."

"I'm so sorry for that. You are the kindest person I know. I apologize." I was very careful not to make the situation about anything other than my deepest apology. "When something like this happens, I worry about the people I love and desperately try to help out. I'm sorry. I love you and Abby more than anything in this world."

"I know that, but you're going to have to convince her of that." He threw a chin her way. "We are good. We will talk later."

"Okay, and if you need anything, I mean *anything*"—money was actually on my mind, and even though I didn't have much, I was willing to give them all I could—"I am here."

"We appreciate that." A long sigh escaped him as he walked away. Before he got into the car and shut the door, he turned back around to look at me one last time.

Abby didn't pay me or Dottie a bit of attention. The tires of the car screeched as she swung it around and zoomed back down the gravel drive.

"Yep. You sure did step in it," Dottie murmured, referring to the situation my snooping had gotten me into with my dearest friend Abby.

CHAPTER 11

Downtown was a little more crowded than it had been earlier. There wasn't an empty picnic table on the grassy median. It was good to see people enjoying the sunshine, lying on blankets without a care in the world. The laughter of children spilled out in echoes from the amphitheater. Their arms were out like airplanes, heads back as they twirled around, giggling with each turn.

None of these tourists knew what had taken place just down the road, and I sure wished I didn't either.

Gert gave me a tense smile when I walked into Trails Coffee. From the looks of it, she was trying to keep her mind off the murder with some customer chitchat. There was always a tickle in the back our minds that said if another person was found murdered in Normal, our business would stop, which meant our livelihoods would be ruined.

There was just one problem with the area we lived. The Daniel Boone National Forest was over seven hundred thousand acres of land, and anyone could drop off a body anywhere. It could take years for someone to discover bones, and then there had to be DNA testing to see if they were even human or not.

Keeping murders quiet and trying to find the killers in the fastest possible way was exactly how we kept things under wraps.

Without disturbing her by saying hello—besides, she already knew why I was there—I slipped past her and headed down the small hall she'd used for storage for many years. In that small room were a desk and a couple of chairs fit for Jerry Truman to open his private-investigation office.

"Knock, knock." I opened the door.

"Oh, thank goodness you're here." Corie was sitting in one of the chairs, and her voice was laced with concern. "I was just telling Hank that you two have to go undercover and figure out which one killed Rick."

Hank's brows furrowed with uncertainty. "We don't even know if one of the dancers might have killed him." Hank would say just about anything to get out of dance class.

"Are you saying you believe one of the people in our dance class killed Ricky? Because I know Bobby Ray and Kirby have alibis." I didn't say they were strong alibis, but they did have ones with witnesses.

Yeah, the witnesses were their significant others, but still, under oath was under oath.

"Don't be silly," she said. I could practically see her lip trembling. "One of the competitors? You two need to go undercover just like your website says and join the competition. You two have chemistry to make this seem like you aren't undercover, unless..." Her voice dropped off like she'd fallen off a ledge. "What about Dottie and, um..." She hesitated. "That handyman of yours."

"Henry and Dottie?" Hank questioned as if it were the most unreasonable couple ever.

"Yes! Undeniable chemistry." Corie sucked in a deep, satisfying breath. "Mae, you can be their photographer, which would get you backstage and into the dressing rooms. A lot of chatter goes on in the dressing rooms."

That wouldn't be too hard to pull off. The National Park Committee did give me that nice camera to use, and I could even take the photos to Violet Rhinehammer. She was the local news reporter and always in search of the next big story.

This whole dance competition was a big story, and I would bet money she'd be at the opening ceremony this afternoon to report on it, especially now with Ricky's death.

"And you-" She pointed at Hank and continued her little scheme. "You can be their manager. Up-and-coming. I can teach them the basic steps, but their chemistry will be off the hook."

A pin-drop silence descended upon the room. Corie looked pleased as pie, but there was a shock factor Hank and I had to get over before we could even process all she'd suggested.

"I don't think Dottie will go for that." My words came out more static than fluid. "Besides, aren't they a little old for this?"

"Age is a number. They have to do it. For the sake of finding justice for Ricky." Her sudden care and concern for him made me pause.

I wasn't saying she killed him, but I also wasn't saying she didn't. The way they argued and fussed at the only dance lesson we'd had was enough motive in my book. She did say that she would get rid of him. What did that mean? The only way to find out...

"How do we know you're not the killer?" My words were met with a drop of Corie's jaw, and she rolled her eyes up to the sky. "You two didn't have the best chemistry at the dance lesson." I continued to use her words against her. "You said you'd get rid of him."

"I have no reason to kill him." She scoffed.

"He was flirting with Felicity. He also flirted with Abby," Hank said. I'd not realized he'd made that observation.

"Flirting? So?" Corie continued to act taken aback as though it were the most unreasonable thing in the world.

"Maybe you're jealous of how he does that and it got to you. I mean, the two of you did leave the sheriff's department at the same time." Hank continued to say things I didn't know but was pretty sure he'd gotten from his granny, whom I still needed to go see in the small hospital in Beattyville.

"I don't care who he sees or brings home as long as we win, and that is clearly out of the picture. My parents will go to the grave when they get word my brother has been killed."

"Your brother?" I asked. Shock riddled me.

"Yes. Wait." She took a couple of steps away from me and Hank. "Did you think Ricky and I were partner partners?"

"By the way he rolled you around his hip and dipped you, dragging his finger down your chin, then your neck, then your sternum, yeah." I sure didn't know any siblings who did those things.

"We are performers. And when you do those types of close dances, there's no better partner than your sibling since there's no chance of us ever being attracted to each other." She looked at me and Hank. "So when I told him I would get rid of him, I meant I'd snag another partner to replace him and send Ricky back home to our parents in Italy."

"Italy?" I asked, as all of her information was being spit at us for the first time, each little tidbit as shocking as the next.

"My parents sent us here for dance school when we were teenagers. We picked up the language fairly quickly, and with good dialect coaches, we lost our Italian accents. When the judge questioned us on it during our citizenship class, he said he had no idea when we spoke to him that we weren't born and raised here in the states." She glanced away. Her face held a flat look. "Ricardo—Ricky, as you know him—fell in love with Kentucky when we came to Louisville for a dance competition.

He loved the hiking here in the Daniel Boone National Forest, which keeps you very fit. It took a lot of convincing on his part to get me to move here, though I knew we could travel just as easily from here as Louisville."

Hank was taking copious notes while I continued to take deeper and deeper interest in her story.

"My full name is Corinna, but it's Corie for short." Her heavily rouged lips lay in a bird-thin line. Her lashes fluttered, trying to dam up the tears floating in her eyes like they were snow globes.

"Gosh. You two just seemed so in sync." I recalled them dancing not only at the dance lesson but at the Red Barn.

"That's the magic between siblings when there's no sexual tension." She made sense. "Are you going to help me or not?"

Hank rubbed his chin, a sure sign he was mulling over what Corie had told us and the facts of the case. Hank really went by the facts, which did make sense, but sometimes, I found the facts were a bit skewed.

The law was based on all the factual things. Yes, Bobby Ray and Kirby fought. Kirby fought with Ricky. Both instances could lead to the death of Ricky, and there were facts that put both men at the crime scene. It was the lesser-known motives that we had yet to discover that gave me the goosebumps.

Those were the leads I would be chasing if I were on the case. But I wasn't. Which was good, because I would spend my time making sure Bobby Ray didn't go down with this ship. Hank could worry about the rest.

"My partner and his wife are on a much-needed vacation." Hank told Corie about Jerry taking Emmalyn, his wife, to the beach as a Valentine's Day present, making me believe Hank wasn't going to take Corie's offer. "I'll do it if and only if Mae will agree to help out."

I had a nagging suspicion Hank had more up his sleeve about the case than he was willing to admit.

Both of them looked at me.

"I, um, well..." Heat rose up in my throat and dampened my armpits. I searched Hank's face to see what he was wanting me to do. His expression hadn't changed. "I guess I can snoop around."

"Then it's settled." Corie pulled the strap of her purse off her shoulder. She unzipped it, sticking her hand inside. "This will do for now."

A wad of cash left her hand and plopped down on Hank's desk.

"I'll be expecting an update every evening." She twisted around to address me. "Mae, I will, in the meantime, have someone come and finish the dance lessons for you. I'm going to need to work with Dottie and Henry one-on-one to get them prepared for the competition. I have a fancy camera in my car to go with your undercover persona."

Corie had it all figured out.

"I don't think you can count on Dottie and Henry." I had to be honest. "I don't think they'll see this the way you are seeing it."

"I've hired you to do the job. It needs to be done properly." She twisted toward the door as if it were a dance move.

"What about Queenie?" I suggested. "I think she'd be more suited for the competition since she has dance experience."

"She has Jazzercise moves." Corie lifted her hands in the air, spreading her fingers apart. She shook them in front of her. "Jazz hands are much different than dance hands." She pulled her fingers in tightly together and did some sort of gesture I was very unfamiliar with. "Plus, I need the chemistry of Dottie and Henry."

"I'm not so sure." I wanted to be clear that she shouldn't

bank on me getting Dottie to play the part. Especially with Henry. Henry, well, he was a different story. He was always up for some fun but possibly with Queenie and not Dottie.

"I have no doubt you'll come through." She exited the door. I followed her to make sure she really left, acting as if I was being a good Southern gal and walking her to the coffee shop door.

"What was that about?" Gert asked as I squeezed my way between the tightly packed customers.

"Something I'm not sure I can pull off," I muttered and headed back to Hank's office, where I found him leaned forward with his elbows propped up on the desk as though contemplating his next move. "Well?"

"Grab your coat." He planted his flat palms on top of the desk and pushed to stand. "We need to go see Granny."

CHAPTER 12

Agnes Swift was a spry eighty-something-year-old woman with short curly grey hair. The only thing that gave her age away was her saggy jowls. Age was no longer determined by hair color. There'd been many young women hikers who'd come to Happy Trails Campground and actually had their hair dyed gray for fashion.

Beat the heck out of me. Before I owned the campground, I'd spent thousands of dollars covering any sort of aging process money could buy, a luxury I had not been able to afforded in a long time. So when I pulled the visor down and took a look at myself in the mirror on the drive to the hospital, I realized what extravagant spa treatments could hide when I saw my crow's feet were starting to deepen.

"You're beautiful." Hank tossed his hand in the air, swiping the edge of the visor and knocking it up. "Now, let's put on a happy face for Granny, and let's not give her any ideas that something is going on."

"She knew about the case though, right? Wasn't she in there when Al brought Bobby Ray and..." My words drifted off after I realized she had gone into the hospital before Ricky was found dead. "Right. I won't say a word." I used my fingers to zip my lips.

We headed through the sliding glass doors of the small hospital, and I followed Hank over to the flower cart. The pale walls of the hospital gave way to florescent lights. The old, yellowing tile had seen much better days, but it appeared clean and shiny. There was no doubt this hospital could use a good makeover, but being a holdover unit, I was sure they didn't want to invest the money into it.

There wasn't a gift shop, but the bouquet Hank picked out would brighten Agnes's day. Anything from Hank would put a great big smile on her face.

"Let's pick two." I picked out another one, and Hank paid for them.

"Granny's room might not be big enough for two." Hank brought his bouquet up to his nose and gave it a sniff as we walked down the hall.

"This one is for the nurses," I told him. "We want Agnes to be getting the best possible care. I'm not above a bribe, and we love flowers."

The sound of our steps hitting the tile as we approached the desk caused the nurses to look up.

"Good morning." I looked both of them in the eyes. "We are here to see Agnes Swift."

"She's in room 105." The petite blond nurse had a button nose and pink lips. She wore a blue pair of scrubs. She had on fake lashes that would make Crissy Lane swoon.

"Thank you for taking such good care of her," I told the nurses and extended the flowers. "We hope these brighten your day."

"That's so sweet of y'all." The young lady took them. The older one got up from in front of the computer and headed to a room behind them with a plaque on the door reading Staff Only. "She's the sweetest ever."

The nurse came back out with a vase in her hands. Obviously, they'd gotten flowers before, but the flowers would put a little color on their counter.

"How is she doing?" Hank asked. When the nurses hesitated, he put his hand on his chest and said, "I'm her grandson and guardian, Hank Sharp."

A beeping echoed behind them. The older nurse checked on it and pushed a button to stop the noise.

"Oh." The young nurse's face lit up. "The detective. She is so proud of you. She talks about you every time I go in there to take her vitals."

The older nurse got up and squinted a smile before she walked around the counter to enter a room with a flashing light above the door. "She's improving. I think she got food poisoning. She should be able to go home later this afternoon or in the morning. Depends on what the doctor says when he does his last set of rounds for the day." She held up a finger and took the phone call ringing in.

We gave her a wave and let her get on with her day.

"See, a little bribery goes a long way." My hand drew down Hank's arm and ended in us holding hands as we made our way to Agnes's room.

"Knock, knock." Hank let go of my hand and used his knuckle to give a couple quick raps on the door. He then pushed the door open just enough for us to pop our heads inside.

Agnes was sleeping.

"What should we do?" He pulled his head back out into the hallway.

"We can leave her flowers on the table next to the bed," I suggested.

He gave a shrug and pushed the door open farther. He winced when it squeaked.

We peeked our heads in again.

"You better get in here." Agnes's voice was like music to my ears. "And you too!" She looked so small sitting in that hospital bed with her arms extended.

"I was so worried about you," Hank told her and sat at the edge of her bed, giving her the flowers before taking her up on her hug.

"Me too." I stood next to him and looked down at her.

"You get over here." She patted the opposite side of the bed for me to join her. "How's my Precious?" She looked up at the bright light and squinted.

"She's great. She really likes having Chester around," Hank teased. "You want him when you get out?"

I fiddled with the light switches on the wall to see which one turned down the lights above her head.

"Heck no. I got rid of you, and now it's the girls. Me and Precious." She winked at him and shifted to me. She put her hand up to the small oxygen device in her nose. "They are making me wear this while I'm in here, but truthfully, I slip it off a lot."

I looked behind her toward the bubbling noise the oxygen was attached to. There was a small plastic box with water in it attached to the hose of the machine she was breathing from. I had no idea what it was but figured it was good for her.

"You keep it in, or they won't release you," Hank warned.

It was so sweet to see his massive hands holding hers so delicately. I glanced around and noticed the adjustable TV table next to her bed holding a piece of dry toast on a paper plate, an empty pill cup, and a plastic bowl with a fountain-drink lid on it, which must've been some sort of broth.

"Do you mind getting me a cup of ice?" she asked Hank. "And a Coke?"

"Why don't you call the nurse?" He reached over to the remote control clipped onto the sheet next to her head.

"No. No." She waved him to stop. "They've got patients to take care of that are way sicker than me. I don't want to take away from them. Please go get me a cup of ice." She didn't necessarily say it as a suggestion but more of a direction. "And a Diet Coke too."

"I'll have to go down to the little cart." He didn't seem to like being sent on an errand.

"Go on before they run out." Agnes was pushing the subject a little too hard, and by Hank's reaction, I could tell he was on to her. "Go on, I said." She one-finger shooed him out the door.

"I want to know every single word she tells you when we leave," he whispered in my ear before he gave me a kiss.

"This is a hospital room, not a hotel," Agnes added with a slight smile of defiance.

"I'm gone. You two ladies can talk about whatever it is you don't want me to hear." Hank shut the door behind him but not before the sounds of beeps and bings from the hallway outside made their echoes into the room.

"Get over here." Agnes pushed herself up a little by her fists then patted the hospital bed.

"I'm not going to sit on your bed," I told her but sat anyway when she gave me a hard look. "If you're worried about Precious, I assure you she's fine."

"No. I'm sure she is. Heck"—she threw a limp wrist at me—"I bet she likes it better there with her mama and Chester than being alone with me."

"I don't think so, but she is fine." I made sure to keep it positive. "Now, what is it you didn't want Hank to hear?"

"This case is a humdinger." She nodded.

"Wait. You mean to tell me you want to talk about Ricky's murder while you're supposed to be getting better?" I asked.

"This—" She took the oxygen out of her nose. "This ain't nothin'." She slipped the small tubes back in then took a deep inhale.

"Yes. Keep those in," I scolded her and took her hand in mine. "Let's talk about getting you better."

"I don't want to talk about that. I want to tell you about this case. There's something funny going on inside that dance competition. And one of them killed that man." The tone of her voice and the fact that she knew about Ricky made me take notice. "Don't look so shocked. It was on the news, and I ain't deaf or dead."

"Hank asked me not to talk to you about it," I confessed.

"And since when have you listened to my grandson?" She gave a snarky grin. "That's why I had him go get me some ice and a Coke."

I laughed. She was going to be just fine.

"I don't know what it is, but there's a lot of competition between them, and I know that because Al went over to the Old Train Station Motel and interviewed some of the dancers. From what I could gather from the notes, they are all cutthroat."

"I came by the department and saw your replacement." I offered a smile, but she didn't take it.

"Huh. Pearl." Agnes's voice was cold and exacting. "She's a youngin'. She doesn't like to answer the dispatch phone right. She isn't loving."

"Loving?" Dispatchers needed to be fast and accurate in order to get Al Hemmer or the park rangers where they needed to go.

"Why, yes. When someone calls in about a hiker missing or someone getting burned by a campfire spark, you've got to tell them it's going to be all right, and sometimes when they have a cut or something, I can talk them into what they need to do and calm them down. Not Pearl." Her neck pulled back, and her head followed. She pursed her lips. "Mmm-mmm. She just rings it on through to Al or whoever answers the phone. That wastes taxpayer dollars, and we need all the dollars we can get to stay in the department we got."

"Is Mayor MacKenzie still talking about moving the sheriff's department?" I asked, changing the subject so I could keep her off the topic of the murder.

Mayor Courtney MacKenzie had seen such a backlash from the residents of Normal about how the population had grown—which was great, but the limited number of employees at the courthouse created much longer lines than the citizens were used to standing in to get things like car tags, property tax information, and the rest of the basic stuff taken care of at a courthouse. Since the sheriff's department took up a big chunk at the back of the building, Mayor MacKenzie had made mention of how she thought it was time the sheriff's department moved out of the courthouse and into its own facility, which would free up space for the government offices to grow.

This was more a political tactic from her since it would look like she took care of the citizens, but when you boiled it down, in the long run, the citizens' taxes would have to pay for a brand-new sheriff's department.

Either way, it was a no-win situation for anyone, and Agnes Swift did not care about it at all.

"I don't know what she's doing, but I do know that you have to get out to the Old Train Station Motel and interview them if you want to get a leg up on Al." Agnes had been such a great contact for me.

Honestly, she should've never done what she'd been doing—accidentally leaving files open on her desk then walking away or, occasionally, actually copying a file and leaving it on the desk, saying she didn't know anything, and walking away, leaving me there to take it. Granted, I was betting it was all illegal, but in the end, my snooping did in fact put a lot of criminals in jail or prison.

"The dancer I hired for the lesson for my campground guests—" I started to tell her.

She drew her hands up to her mouth in delight and squealed, "I forgot. Tell me." She was smiling so big. "Does Hank hate them?" She was asking about Hank's apprehension about taking dance lessons.

"He's not a big fan." I laughed and followed up with "But he's a big fan of moi." I put my hand on my chest. "So he participated as much as Hank could participate."

Both of us laughed. Both of us knew Hank very well.

"Really." I put my hand back on her fragile and thin fingers. "I don't want you to worry about anything. You need to get better. If not for you then for me and Hank. And Precious," I added when I realized I'd forgotten her fur baby she loved so dearly.

"The only way I know to get better is to know you are out there doing something." Her jowls clenched, making her skin wiggle a smidgen. Her eyes narrowed slightly.

Agnes was not going to let anything go until I agreed.

"If it's any comfort to you, Corie has asked Hank to look into it, which means we have leads to follow until you get out of the hospital." I watched her mouth curl into an infectious grin that set the tone.

Off she went.

"You also need to look into that Marshall man." Her voice rose an octave as her mind set aflame brainstorming the possible suspects. I decided not to tell her about what Kirby had told me. The longer she talked, the visibly weaker she was. Her voice was softening. "What about the partner? She could have a motive and came to you to cover up the facts."

"True. I have thought about it," I murmured at the good possibility of the sibling rivalry that brought out the competition. "How long have they been partners?" I questioned out loud. "Was he about to achieve some sort of higher status in the dance world?"

"Maybe leaving her behind?" Agnes's eyes grew. "No partner likes to be left behind."

"There's more than that." I gulped and knew I shouldn't tell her, but I spit it out. All of it out. "They are siblings."

I continued to tell her about how they moved to the United States and they'd both gotten to Normal. There wasn't much I knew about the dance business, other than that it was big business and with these television competition shows, it'd gotten even bigger.

"Where was she the night of the murder?" Agnes asked.

"I don't know." My voice cut to silence.

A chill swept along the cold tile floor of the hospital room when Hank opened the door. Goose bumps carried up my legs and finally found a home around the back of my neck.

"We don't even know the time of death yet." I sighed and stood up. "With you in here, Pearl surely wasn't going to give me the initial coroner's report."

"I am going to go see Colonel Holz this afternoon." Hank joined in on the conversation, though he looked at me under hooded eyes, letting me know he didn't like what he'd walked in on.

He handed Agnes her drink and also a chocolate bar.

"You sure do know how to butter up your granny, boy." She reached out to grab his hand. "I love you so much, Hank."

"I love you too, Granny." Hank bent down and hugged her.

When he stood up, I noticed his wet eyes but turned away so

he didn't see me notice or see the scared look on my face. The thought of Hank losing Agnes was something that I could see on his face was just now hitting him. I wasn't even sure if the thought had ever crossed his mind.

I was guessing not.

"I'm going to step outside and give Mary Elizabeth a call while you two say goodbye." I hugged Agnes. When I passed Hank, I ran my fingernail along his arm. "Granny needs her sleep so her body can rest and get stronger. We need you home." I gave her a look, and she wagged her head. "And keep that oxygen on."

I turned the door handle all the way so that when I closed the door, it closed gently. Headed down the hall, I pulled my phone from my pocket and dialed Mary Elizabeth.

"Oh my stars." She sounded worried on the other end. "I've been waiting for you to call me all day. I heard about Agnes, and well, I figured you had your hands full."

"How did you know I was at the hospital?" I asked and sat down in one of the pleather chairs in the lobby. The arms boasted cracks in the material, and pieces had been picked off.

"Did you forget that I raised you?" She snorted. "You might try to forget your raisings, but there's some of that etiquette and manners class still inside of you."

Mary Elizabeth was right. No matter how much I tried to forget all of those classes she made me attend after she became my foster mom then adoptive mother, she knew some of the rules still stayed with me.

Just like she knew if someone I loved dearly was in the hospital, I'd be there.

"How is she, May-bell-ine?" Her Southern accent drew out my full name.

"She looks frail, and for the first time, I saw Hank worried about her." I left the words there for her to take in. "We can talk about that when I get there."

"You're stopping by?" Excitement infused her voice.

"I was thinking about having Hank drop me off, then maybe you can take me to my car downtown." I had ridden with Hank in his truck.

"Of course. I'd do anything to spend some time with you. Plus, I can't wait to hear about the dance lessons."

"Mm-hmm, I know that tone," I said.

"What tone?" she asked.

"The tone implying these lessons will come in handy on my wedding day." It was no big secret that Mary Elizabeth was counting the passing days as I got older by the minute, which was a death sentence in the South. "I've already had a wedding day, and I'm not going to have another big one."

"I wasn't at the last one, so it doesn't count," she snapped back, reminding me of my first marriage to Paul West, who not only went to prison for pulling off one of the biggest Ponzi schemes in the United States but also was murdered over it. It was a memory I tried hard to forget, even though he had deeded the campground over to me. At the time, I thought I was going to be able to sell Happy Trails for a pretty penny. I couldn't even get a tarnished nickel for the shape it was in, so the next thing I knew, I was fixing it up and actually coming to love Normal.

Never left. Never planned to.

"I'll see you soon." I hurried off the phone when I heard footsteps coming down the hallway and looked up to see Hank.

"How is Mary Elizabeth?" he asked on our way out the sliding glass doors.

"You can see for yourself." I slid my hand down his arm and clasped our fingers together. "Do you mind dropping me off on our way back? That way, I can talk to her about Bobby Ray, and you can head on over to see Colonel Holz."

CHAPTER 13

The Milkery Dairy Farm was a business Mary Elizabeth had decided to purchase with Dawn Gentry. Mary Elizabeth came to visit me one day and decided to stay, and Dawn was a tourist who fell in love with Normal as much as I did and decided to stay and become Mary Elizabeth's business partner.

It was actually a good move on both of their parts. Mary Elizabeth had that Southern-hospitality touch that made everyone feel so welcomed and at home. On the other hand, Dawn was the financial and business wizard, so she took care of all of those items that kept the Milkery afloat.

After running it as the dairy farm, they also decided to renovate the old mansion home on the farm and turn it into a bed-and-breakfast—a brilliant move since there were very few places, other than a camper or tent, to stay in the Daniel Boone National Park. They were always booked, and by the looks of all the cars in the parking lot, this week was no different.

"Valentine's Day." Hank leaned over as though he were reading my mind.

"Speaking of Valentine's..." I let the sentence dangle.

"Don't you worry. I've got it covered." He gave me a peck on the lips before he jumped out of the truck to hustle over to my door and open it like a good Southern gentleman. "I'll run in and say hello."

Large silos towered over the property with the farm's name printed on each of them. The cows were all huddled together on one side of the Kentucky post fence, and the chickens were on the other side. Their coop was nicer than my camper. Mary Elizabeth insisted they be pampered because she felt like they laid better-tasting eggs. She'd even gone as far as putting a rocking chair in there with them and reading them a book a night.

I let her be. It kept her busy, and she loved it.

We headed around to the back of the house, where the kitchen door was open but the screen shut.

"It's a little too chilly to have this door open," I said on my way in, getting a whiff of something sweet that made my mouth water.

Hank stopped. He lifted his chin in the air and sucked in.

"Don't tell me you're making raspberry-cream sugar cookies." His lips fell into a grin.

"I won't tell you." She whipped around holding a tray filled with the delicious double-stacked sugar cookies with the raspberry filling in the middle. "I'll give you a few." Her Southern drawl streamed out of her mouth.

The strand of pearls looked so nice against her hot-pink cardigan and lime-green, white, and hot-pink Lily Pulitzer ankle khakis.

"Weee-doggie." Hank nearly bowled me over to get across the kitchen.

She handed him the tray and pointed for him to take it over to the large farm table, where she'd already put out glasses filled to the tops with ice, a big pitcher of her homemade lemonade next to them.

I shut the door behind me.

"I had to leave the door open, or the smell of all this sugar and ingredients would find its way onto my gut." She patted her belly. "I think I outdid myself on this batch."

"Hey, guys." Dawn Gentry rounded the corner from the hallway that led to the hospitality room of the bed-and-breakfast. "I thought I smelled something good."

I pushed back my thick, curly honey hair when I got hair envy from looking at Dawn's laid-back pixie-cut style. She was so cool in her skinny jeans and leather jacket. It was an outfit she could easily pull off.

Not me.

"All the way to the office?" Mary Elizabeth secretly loved how the smells of her baking fluttered all over the Milkery. It was the guests with their complimentary comments that made Mary Elizabeth shine. "Good. I hope everyone starts coming down. It's been quiet here this week. We are full up, but they don't want to leave their rooms."

"I told you it's Valentine's week. The same thing happened last year. Remember?" Dawn sat down and picked at the edges of her black pixie haircut before she decided on a cookie.

She sat back in the chair with her leg up under her.

"If you sit like that, you're gonna have one leg shorter than the other," Mary Elizabeth warned. It was one of her old wives tales she told me growing up. "Besides, it's not ladylike."

"Whoever said I was a lady?" Dawn asked. "I'm tough. Remember, I'm from the city."

"Speaking of which"—I turned my attention to Dawn—"how was the city?"

Dawn was from New York and had gone back a week after Christmas to visit.

"It was nice. I'd forgotten about the hustle and bustle." She stuffed the cookie in her mouth. "I actually sorta missed it when I got back."

"Don't be going and getting no sneaky ideas up in your head about leaving me," Mary Elizabeth warned and brought over a to-go baggie filled with cookies. She'd already written Hank's name on it like someone was going to steal his bag.

"Thank you." He wagged one in the air at me. "You need to learn to make these." He popped it into his mouth.

"You can learn," I told him. I was many things but a baker I was not. I could help out, but not take the lead. I was a blue-ribbon winner in the tasting department.

Hank's phone chirped. He took it out of his jeans pocket to see who it was. "Colonel." He got up but not without popping in one more cookie. "Gotta go." He walked over and kissed me. "I'll let you know what I find out."

"Find out?" Mary Elizabeth's curiosity spiraled upward. "Find out what?" She took a seat where Hank had been sitting.

"The dead body from Grassel's Garage turned out to be a murder, and his sister has hired Hank to look into it." I tried not to give too much detail about Ricky's case because I was here to find out if she knew anything about Bobby Ray and Abby's financial situation.

It might appear like I was being nosy and snooping into their affairs, but it was definitely the opposite. Since I'd made a home here and ran the campground, I'd gotten fairly good in the finance department and at running a business. I could help them out. I loved Bobby Ray and Abby so much that I'd do just about anything for them.

"Since Agnes isn't at work, Hank is going through the proper channels to get information about the autopsy. I wanted to ask you if you knew anything about Bobby Ray and Abby?" I asked Mary Elizabeth.

"Know anything? I know a lot." Mary Elizabeth stood up and

busied herself by fiddling with a cleaning rag before she decided to wipe down the cabinets.

Dawn and I looked at each other. Dawn shrugged.

"I'm going to go back to the office," Dawn whispered before she disappeared from where she'd come.

"And if you think Bobby Ray had anything to do with that boy's death—" My foster mother started in on me before I could even defend myself.

"I don't." I grabbed a white napkin from the holder in the middle of the table and waved it in the air as if I were surrendering.

"Oh Mae, honey. I'm so sorry. I've been so worried." Her brows knotted. She came back over to the table and sat with one cheek on the chair, all cockeyed like. She plucked the napkin from my hands and dabbed her eyes with it right before she covered her face with her hands.

"Worried about them?" My inkling that something was wrong was now confirmed.

"Yes. That big ole house of theirs." Mary Elizabeth lifted her face out of her palms and gave a slight shake of her head that hinted at something along the lines of disappointment. "They never should've bought it. Who on earth needs such a big house in a fancy neighborhood when they are starting out?"

"I think they got a pretty good deal on it." There was no need to remind Mary Elizabeth how there'd been a murder in the home and the realtor had been having a hard time getting someone to purchase it due to that little-known fact.

"It's got upkeep, utilities." She lifted a finger and shook it at me. "Which aren't cheap. Besides, did Abby tell you?"

"No." I shook my head. "They had an argument, and apparently, Bobby Ray believes Abby is spending a lot of money on the house and other things."

"She sure is. Breaking my baby too." Mary Elizabeth's mama

bear was coming out. Though she wasn't technically my or Bobby Ray's real mother, she still had the attitude and possessiveness of one.

"What if he's breaking her?" I suggested but quickly receded when Mary Elizabeth's eyes snapped to mine. "I think they both make pretty decent money, and it takes two. Bobby Ray's equipment he uses for the shop can't be cheap."

"And she wastes her money on buying more Tupperware to sell when no one ain't buying or using Tupperware now that you can get the plastic ones you can throw away." Mary Elizabeth huffed.

"Throw away," I repeated.

"Yes. I said throw away."

"I think we might have a solution to Abby's income problem with her Tupperware." I smiled and grabbed a cookie for each hand. "Do you mind driving me to get my car?"

"Only if on the way over, you tell me what's going through that little head of yours." She wasn't about to let me leave without me agreeing to let her in.

And I did just that.

"You think this is going to work?" she asked.

"I do. Abby loves the Daniel Boone National Forest and so does Bobby Ray. It has to work." I jumped out of the car and couldn't wait to let Abby in on my solution.

CHAPTER 14

"Just wait a minute." I tried to stop Abby from digging into one of the many plastic containers Coke Ogden, the owner of Old Train Station Motel, had set out for her to go through to help decorate the barn venue center. "I'm sorry I even implied Bobby Ray could've done something to Ricky. I'm even more sorry I stuck my nose into your financial affairs, but I think I have a solution."

I had gotten my camera out of my trunk, the one the committee had given me to take on my trail excursion, and hung it around my neck. I lifted it up and acted like I was going to take a photo of Abby.

She gave me a flat look.

"I'm undercover, and I need you to help." That didn't even seem to sway her. "I'm hoping to get Dottie and Henry to pretend to be dance partners so we can get on the inside."

If that wasn't going to entice her to jump in with both feet, I wasn't sure what was.

An apology.

"I'm sorry." I begged and pleaded. Her face softened, a little.

"Even Mary Elizabeth thinks my idea is a great idea." Apparently, I hadn't said the right thing.

She tossed the bundle of paper hearts from her arms back into the container.

"You told Mary Elizabeth?" Abby's eyes grew. "I can't believe you'd do that."

"What? She already knew something was going on. I guess Bobby Ray..." I stopped talking as I watched Abby's left eyebrow slowly arch. "I mean, I went to her for some advice on how to fix this." I gestured between the two of us. "I'm not good at this sort of thing. You know that." I reminded her of when I first came to town. "Remember you hugging me the first time I ever laid eyes on you? We hug around here. That's what you told me."

The memory made her smile. A snort escaped her. "We aren't in trouble. It's that I need to stop spending money on making our house a perfect home and find another job outside of Tupperware if I do want to spend the extra money." She reached back down into the container and took the hearts back out. "Here, if you're going to tell me your grand plan, you might's well help."

My phone rang. I put the paper hearts underneath my armpit and nudged my phone out of my pocket for a peek when I saw it was Hank.

"Let me grab this," I told her and stepped aside for a minute. "Hey, what's the word?"

"The word is—" Music blared over the surround-sound speakers, making it very difficult for me to hear.

"Hold on!" I yelled into the phone and put the hearts on the floor. I made my way out of the barn without being hit by the dancing couples twirling around the big open space. "Goodness. You have to be careful on the dance floor," I said once I safely made it out the barn.

"Huh?" Hank asked.

"I was in the barn venue, talking to Abby when you called, which was also when the dancers were starting their practice for tonight's performance." It was opening night for the competition.

"Don't leave. I need to talk to Corie. According to Colonel, Ricky died between the hours of eleven p.m. and one a.m. The only prints they found were Felicity's, on the button where y'all lowered the car lift."

My mind circled back to Felicity.

"Where was Corie between the hours of eleven and one?" Hank asked.

"Are you thinking she killed her own brother?" I asked, knowing we'd talked about it after leaving Granny Agnes in the hospital. On our ride back to the Milkery, I did tell him about Granny mentioning Corie as a possibility.

Instead of standing in front of the barn Coke had turned into an event venue, I strolled around the field between the barn and the hotel as I listened to Hank. This was one of the prettiest views in all of Normal. Coke had bought the old train station and transformed it into the ten-room motel. The massive concrete station was beautiful, framed by the dramatic backdrop of the mountains of the national park. Coke Ogden had a hit on her hands from the get-go. The set of trails beginning on the back of her property were some of the hardest climbs of the area. Those were the most appealing to tourists who came to Normal for the hiking. The motel made the perfect place for those hikers to get a good night's sleep and then head out in the early morning. Only having ten rooms meant she was always booked, especially since the café was a popular place for locals to eat.

Right in the middle of the Old Train Station Motel was a domed, circular, open courtyard area with six massive concrete pillars holding up a dramatic patina metal roof with a rooster weathervane.

"I'm not sure," Hank said, answering my question, "but I do know Ricky was on target to participate in this year's Royals Dance Competition." Hank was using lingo I had no idea about.

"Royals Dance Competition?" I tried not to smile when I said it.

There was some commotion coming from the courtyard, and when I glanced up, I could only see Coke talking to someone.

Coke had always been an odd bird. She wore her hair in a sixties style parted down the middle with the ends flipped up. She usually wore different headbands to keep her hair out of her face, and today, she'd chosen a pink one and a similar-colored scarf she tied around her neck. She was a tiny thing too. Her birdlike features and small frame went well with each other, but her heart was the largest part of her body.

I had no idea who she was talking to, but pink long-sleeved, bell-shaped sleeves waved in the air as she talked with her hands.

"Yeah. It's actually a pretty huge deal for the Queen." I could hear a male talking, but when Dottie and Henry appeared next to Coke and Corie, I actually stopped listening to Hank to see if I could tell what was going on. "But get this. Corie is already in the competition. Both of them have tickets to go compete in England. This competition at the Old Train Station is really just for them to practice, and from what I heard when I called the organizer, the siblings are pretty competitive. Corie has always been a winner but never won the title of Royal Dance Champion, and she's been three years in a row. According to what I've found, Ricky was the front-runner, and it was the first time he's been eligible."

"Hank, let me call you back." I hung up the phone and trotted up to the motel courtyard.

"I am not one bit happy about this, May-bell-ine." Smoke rolled out of Dottie's mouth. The lines around her lips from smoking all these years deepened with her growl. "I do not appreciate being told I will lose my job if I don't participate in this little scheme."

"I never said you'd lose your job." Corie stomped.

Henry stood there, silent, with an amused look on his face.

"It sure did seem like it." Dottie dropped the cigarette on the ground and used the toe of her shoe to snuff it out. "'Dottie, I went to see Mae and Hank, and they said you have to go undercover,'" Dottie mocked in a high voice like Corie's. "I don't have to do nothin'! Do you hear me, Mae-bell-ine? And I'm no detective either."

"I don't think Hank and I said that. We listened to Corie and her ideas, and someone going undercover is a great idea. In fact, Hank and I are also going undercover," I said. "I'm your photographer, and Hank is your manager. So neither of you will really be dancing. It's just for lookies."

"Lookies, huh?" Dottie gave me the side-eye.

"Yeah. Lookies." I shrugged. "This thing will be wrapped up in no time." My eyes slid past Dottie's shoulder when Hank pulled up in the parking lot of the motel. Our eyes caught on each other when he looked out the windshield.

Henry sat there, smiling, not a care in the world. His toothless grin was adorable.

"Who is at the office?" I asked.

"No one. Corie said he and I had to practice." She flung a hand, hitting Henry in the arm.

"And you do. Even though what Mae says is true, you still have to go in there and dance." Corie was insistent. "Let's go."

Dottie's apprehensiveness kept her back with me. Henry, he had no opinion. He took a giddyup and followed Corie through the courtyard and across the field.

"I can't believe you've roped me into this," Dottie snarled. "I mean, with him."

"Henry?" I questioned. "He's harmless. Besides, Corie thinks you two have chemistry."

"You've got to be kiddin' me. Henry thinks the movie *Deliverance* is a romantic comedy." She and I both grinned.

"I know you love sleuthing. And I'm hoping to get all the Laundry Club Ladies together to help. Abby is in there putting up decorations for Coke, and Betts is still cleaning the motel rooms, so I've yet to talk to them." Betts had a cleaning side hustle, which included cleaning the rooms at the motel when guests requested them or when they checked out.

"From what I understand, Queenie is going to assist with some of the dance costumes since a couple from her Jazzercise class is in the competition. So look at it as something we'd do as a group and not just you and Henry." I really wanted her to give it her best shot.

"I am a good dancer." She patted her hips. "Especially since I got these fixed."

Dottie had hip surgery a couple years ago, and she'd really recovered well.

"I can't believe something like Henry Bryant being a pretend dance partner has stumped you so much," I said. "Maybe you do have a little inkling of something for him." I winked.

"You've lost your ever-lovin' mind, Mae West." She shook her head and headed for the barn as Hank walked up.

"Why did you hang up so fast?" Hank asked and carried a briefcase.

"Dottie was fussing, and I needed to put a stop to it before any of the dancers saw her. You know, undercover and all." There wasn't a need to go over all the details about Dottie and what I thought could be a little attraction to Henry.

I could be way off, but Dottie sure was acting strange, something I'd never seen in her.

"Now, what were you saying about Corie and the Royal-whatever competition?" I asked him.

On our walk through the field, he recounted what he'd told me on the phone when I wasn't really listening. "She has a pretty good motive to have really done a number on him. It's a fierce competition." He glanced at me. "I can see you're not buying it."

"Not fully. I mean, I understand that she's going full hog on trying to help us solve the murder since she hired us, which is a little suspect, but I'm not sure she could pull that off." I realized we didn't have a true alibi for her.

When we stepped into the barn, Corie was talking to a few of the dancers, who seemed to be consoling her. Henry and Dottie were off to the side, putting on dancing shoes. Abby was on a ladder hanging those hearts.

I lifted the camera to my face and clicked a few photos to make it seem like I was doing my job. "I'm just taking a few action shots," I told Dottie when she gave me an annoyed look. "We have reason to believe Ricky could've been killed by another dancer. Possible competition motive. And I want to get some of these dancers in the photo so we can look them up."

"If you ask me..." she started to say then took a minute to look around. She leaned over and whispered, "Corie seems to really be playing the part so hard, I can't help but think she's covering something up."

"Mary Elizabeth said the same thing." I shifted my focus to Corie, who was still surrounded by the other dancers. One in particular caught my interest.

He was about six foot, four inches, had coal-black hair, and was of what I'd consider to be Italian descent. He seemed to be peering at her intently. The other dancers fell away, leaving Corie alone with the lean and muscular man.

She said something to him. He made a slight gesture with his right hand before he turned on his heels and strode to the door.

"Did you hear me?" Dottie looked past me to see what I was gawking at.

"Yeah. I'll be right back," I told her over my shoulder.

"Wait! Get these photos and get me out of here!" There was an urgency in her voice, but I would deal with that in a few minutes.

There was definitely something going on between Corie and the other dancer. This would be my opportunity to ask him some questions, because she obviously didn't tell me or Hank about any relationships she had within the dancer community, which made me question her even more.

The sun hung over the early spring day, warming the chilly morning into a nice afternoon. It was deceiving when you hiked around here. With the sun hanging overhead, you'd think it would be nice and warm. It was opposite in the forest, where the trees kept the trails nice and shaded and therefore cool.

There were several hikers making their way to the trailheads across the field behind the motel, making it difficult for me to find the man after I stepped outside the barn. I lifted my hand over my brows to shade the brightness when I heard a shuffling coming from the side of the other barn that housed the horses Coke kept for the horse trail rides she offered.

There was a corral attached to the back of the barn where the horses were able to get some exercise, eat, drink water, and socialize between rides rather than stay in their stalls. I noticed the dancer had made his way over there. He hung on the fence with his hand out, offering a handful of grass to the horse, clicking his tongue for the horse to come feed.

I didn't know a ton about horses, but I'd been in this barn a time or two, so I knew enough about feeding them and where Coke kept their preferred snacks.

"Here." I had taken a small bag of the food from just inside the barn and walked over to the dancer. "They don't necessarily want to eat grass all the time, but they will always want this special treat."

As soon as Rosa heard the bag, she trotted over.

"That's Rosa, and I'm Mae." I opened the bag of feed and took out a handful, extending it over the top rung of the fence for Rosa to nibble up. "Go ahead," I encouraged when I noticed he was apprehensive.

"I've never fed a horse." I couldn't say his accent was Italian, but I knew it wasn't native to Kentucky or even the United States.

"All you have to do is grab a handful and extend your fingers all the way out." I took a handful more and showed him. "Flat palm. Just like this."

"Just like that, huh?" The dancer smiled. "Sergie. My name is Sergie." He was smiling from ear to ear. "You are a photographer for the older couple?"

"Yes." Oh gosh. I sure hated to lie, but technically, I could say I was Dottie and Henry's photographer.

While Sergie continued to give Rosa more food, I patted her snoot, down her back, and raked her mane with my fingers.

"May I?" I asked and held my camera up.

"Sure. I'd love to have some photos of me with Rosa." He turned and immediately flashed those pearly whites.

He'd definitely done photo shoots before, I thought to myself.

"How do you want me?" He'd asked a technical question.

"Just be natural." I didn't know any photography lingo or poses, but he didn't seem to question my response.

"Natural" to Sergie was leaning into the fence with a handful of horse food extended, his chin turned slightly upward and a huge smile on his face.

"How long have you been a dancer?" I asked and snapped away, adding in a few "Oh that's a good one" for good measure to keep his mind on the smiling and Rosa so he didn't think my line of questioning was odd.

"All of my life. It was a way of life in my country." He twisted to the other side, and I hurried around him to get some more photos.

It was like Rosa knew what I was doing. She played along so well, even giving Sergie a little nudge with her nose.

"Did you get that one?" He was excited.

"I sure did." I turned the fancy camera around and showed him the screen. I used my thumb to cover up the little stamp that read, *Property of Daniel Boone National Forest*.

His eyes grew big as laughter expelled from him.

"Did you know Ricky, the dancer who passed away?" I asked.

His face stilled, his skin pulled taut over the elegant ridges of his cheekbones.

"I'm sorry. You seem to know him. It's just that my couple, Dottie and Henry, as you can see are a little older, and there were some rumblings about it." I shrugged. "Why don't you put one foot up on the bottom rung, lean your body into the fence, and look Rosa in the eyes."

"Rosa." I clicked my tongue. She was reading my mind.

"If you are a photographer, how do you know this horse?" He'd caught me.

How could I be so careless?

"We are from here. Technically, I'm not a professional photographer, but my friends really wanted to do the dance competition, so they asked me to take photos since I do it for the national park." I swallowed another lie. "I take tourist photos. And the owner of this motel does a lot of mini shoots with her guests. She hires me a lot." I found myself rambling. I gritted my teeth to stop my mouth from talking.

"That is a very cool job to have." He acted as if he bought it. "I do think you look in shape."

"Thank you." He made me blush. "I guess I'm worried about Dottie and Henry. I mean, if people are dying because they are so competitive, I just want to look out for them."

"Why? Are they that good?" he asked.

"Please?" I asked because I didn't quite understand what he'd said.

"Please what?" he asked, brows raised.

"We say 'please' when we need you to repeat something instead of saying 'What did you say?'" I laughed, realizing I was going to have to explain a little. "It just sounds nicer to say please."

"You Southern people are funny creatures." He gave Rosa a pat on the head between her eyes before he brushed his hands off. "I've taken enough of a break."

"About the murder?" I asked again in hopes he'd give me a few more minutes.

"Yes. I knew him. He was very competitive. He had been trying to make it in this business a long time. He thought he'd gotten a great partner a few years ago but ended up he wasn't great for her. She didn't care about the... mmm, shall I say, art." Rosa nudged his arm. "Okay. Okay. I will give you more."

Rosa was going to get a big treat from me. She was instrumental in keeping Sergie here for more questions.

"You'd think if you put your body through all this work, you'd love the art." I thought it was a pretty good comeback to follow up with a question. "What did she enjoy about it?"

"She wanted to do that American dancing show, and she wanted the fame, not the hard work. She was very pretty and charming. People naturally liked her but not Ricardo. He was hellbent on dragging her name through the mud, as you say here in America." He tsked. "You Americans can be very ruthless."

"So, do you think she killed him?" I asked.

"I wouldn't be surprised, or any of the others' toes he's stepped on." He took a deep breath and stepped back from the fence. "Including his recent partner."

"The dance partner he did have—do you know her name?" I asked.

"Tatiana," he whispered as if it were bad to say her name out loud.

"Were you and Ricky on good terms?" I asked, disguising my face with the help of the camera. I used the lens to zoom in on his face to get his reaction.

"We were friendly. He had a very possessive quality to him. He was very particular when he and his partner danced. He had to have all of their outfits fitted perfectly. But you should know most of those little details free our minds so we only have to worry about the dancing in competition." He talked as though I truly knew the industry, but I had no clue.

"Outfits perfect?" I wanted to know more.

"Yes. You know your Dottie, is it?" He waited until I confirmed. "Dottie is, how do I say—older and a little saggier."

"Don't tell her that," I warned.

"Outfits wouldn't fit her bum as they would fit your bum." He leaned a little to his right as though he were getting a view of my backside. "And when we twirl..." He grabbed my hand and twirled me, and before I knew it, he had completely dipped me back.

Our noses touched.

"The world would've seen your tush, and it wouldn't be pretty in the wrong outfit." His breath was hot to my cheek.

My mouth dried.

"Sergie!" The call was from a woman in a dance outfit. Her accent was American. "It's our turn!" She waved for him to come. "You can flirt later!"

"See. Everyone thinks I flirt." He winked. "I'm coming, Di," he called out to the woman before he lifted me to the upright position, dropping my hands from his. "Please get with me so I can see your photos." He sashayed off, stopping halfway to the other barn.

"Yeah." I smiled and lifted my chin, shook my hair, and cleared my throat. "Will do."

"You Americans are funny people." He snickered and rounded the corner of the other barn.

"You did good." I gave Rosa another handful of feed. "But we really didn't get all the answers we needed."

She nudged me with the tip of her nose.

"You're right. It's a start." I gave her one last pat on her neck before I went to put the snack back where I'd found it.

"I see you met Sergie." The voice from inside the horse barn came from a shadow before Corie stepped out. "You have good form. Maybe I asked the wrong woman to be Henry's dance partner."

"I thought you were giving them a lesson." As much as I wanted to think Corie didn't kill her brother, I kept distance between us.

"Dottie needed a smoke break." She smiled. "Did Sergie give you any insight?"

I hesitated.

She noticed.

"I am paying for your services." She played her upper hand.

"You paid for Hank's services. I'm just the girlfriend," I noted and turned to leave the barn so I could go find either Hank or Abby. I had lingering conversations with both of them that needed to be finished.

"You think I killed my own brother." She was much more observant than I'd given her credit for.

I swirled around and shoved a strand of my curly hair behind my ear.

"When was the last time you saw your brother?" I asked.

"The night of his death." She stared at me.

"I mean the exact time." If she wanted hardball, I was willing to play that game.

"After we left the sheriff's department, I dropped him by here, and I went back to the bed-and-breakfast."

"He stayed here?" I asked. "You stayed where?"

"The Milkery." She smiled. "How do you think I got Hank's name after I got word my brother was killed?"

"Mary Elizabeth," I said but kept to myself that Corie was her number-one suspect. Then I wondered why Mary Elizabeth didn't tell me Corie was staying there.

CHAPTER 15

"Good evening, and welcome to this year's dance competition championship." The gold-and-silver backdrop at the front of the venue at the Old Train Station Motel glittered with elegant vibes. "My name is Tatiana. And I can't imagine a better comeback tour starting tonight!"

The applause was so loud, the roar of the crowd made it hard to hear her even though she was speaking into a microphone. There was a long banquet table located on each side of the podium with four people in fancy black-and-white tie attire seated at each. The tables were dressed in gold cloth that hung down to the ground and silver knotted fabric that scalloped in the front.

"Did she say her name was Tatiana?" I nudged Abby, who was sitting at a round table with me, Hank, Bobby Ray, and the rest of the Laundry Club Ladies, minus Dottie. Dottie was standing with Henry in the wings of the dance floor, looking as nervous as a cat in a roomful of rocking chairs.

"She did." Abby's eyes grew. "Didn't you tell me Sergie told you Ricky's last partner before Corie was Tatiana?"

"Yes." I gave a solid nod and looked back at the woman.

"Comeback tour?" Abby shook her head. "How convenient."

"Too convenient if you ask me." I sucked in a deep breath and let the long sigh out my nose.

My eyes shifted. I looked around at all the other dancers. Everyone was smiling so brightly, but I knew the real feelings behind those fake smiles. Over the last twenty-four hours, I'd grown to realize the competition was stiff, and jealousy was rampant between every single dancer here. That was the emotion hidden behind their lined lips and pearly-white teeth that glistened more the than mirror ball hanging from the middle of the ceiling.

"I never thought I'd be launching the tour from the Daniel Boone National Forest or, as locals call it, the holler." The way the woman's accent turned to hick curled my stomach.

I leaned forward, wanting to absorb every single word Tatiana said. Then I realized I could take pictures.

"Where are you going?" Betts asked when I jumped up.

"To snoop." I grabbed the strap of my camera off the back of my chair and lifted it in a gesture to her.

I made my way up to the front of the podium and hunkered down like I'd seen photographers do at press conferences. I snapped several photos of Tatiana.

She was gorgeous, almost too pretty if that was possible. Her cream dress had lines of diamonds, or what looked like diamonds, zigzagging in a diagonal pattern. The hem landed perfectly at her toe line, where the tips of her perfectly polished blush toenails gave their own seductive peep show. The body-hugging dress complimented her long neckline, where the bun of her blond hair was neatly tucked at the nape.

The more angles I could get in my photos of her, the easier it would be when I uploaded them to the computer to quickly grab a match from what I hoped was a nice little footprint on the World Wide Web. I also hoped to get some photos confirmed from Ricky's social media accounts.

"I want to wish everyone tonight good luck. Put your best foot forward, and as we say in the business, break a leg but don't break a leg, really."

She waited for the applause to die down.

"The stakes are high. It's the last competition for you to get your numbers up so you can compete in the Royal Dance Competition, the highest competition you'll ever compete in." She sucked in a deep breath, exuding confidence. With a smug look and her chin lifted high, she continued. "The winner will go to London, England, where you will be performing for the Queen and her family. Such a prestigious honor to represent the United States in such an amazing, amazing opportunity!"

That must've been the big band's cue to start the music. The mirror ball began swirling, and flickers of light danced across the floor, signaling all the dancers to emerge—Dottie and Henry included.

I moved out of the way just in time for a couple to twirl around me, the beads of her dance skirt whacking me in the face and almost taking an eye out.

They all moved in a choreographed dance that I recognized as the one Corie had been working on with Dottie and Henry. It was like you'd see in the movies. Everyone had these complex expressions in their eyes before they melted into huge smiles and arced brows.

Not Dottie.

Her face was as blank and flat as could be. Henry, he was smiling so big, and his head was bobbing back and forth to the music as he tried to twirl Dottie.

I continued to click photos of everyone dancing and in the

crowd, really playing up the part before I made it over to the shadow of the wall closest to Dottie and Henry.

With a watchful eye looking through the lens, I noticed Corie and Tatiana on the opposite side of the room. I used my hand to manually zoom the lens in on them, snapping a few close-ups. Tatiana had lifted a finger at Corie. Corie stood there with her hands on her hips, jutting her face in and out of Tatiana's personal space. Both ladies were saying something through gritted teeth, though Tatiana kept a smile on her face, well aware people may be looking at her.

She was definitely keeping her composure much better than Corie was. Tatiana gave a few exaggerated head nods, as if she weren't agreeing with what Corie had to say, before Corie stomped away.

In a quick move, Sergie had taken Tatiana in his arms. The jewels on her dress twinkled, making it hard distinguish whether the glistening reflections of light on the ceiling, walls, and floors were from the mirror ball or her dress.

Tatiana and Sergie was a striking pair, but I wondered why he wasn't dancing with his partner. My eyes squinted around the dark room, looking for her, and that was when I saw her talking to Hank. Hank looked so handsome in his tuxedo. He leaned against the back wall with his hands tucked into his pants pockets. Sergie's partner, Di, leaned into his ear. His head nodded as she talked.

I turned back and focused on the couple everyone had seemed to make plenty of room for on the dance floor—Tatiana and Sergie. They looked like they'd been a dance couple for years.

My mind raced with thoughts of suspicion about Tatiana's timing for a comeback tour coinciding with Ricky's death. This was awfully coincidental.

I glanced to the back of the room at Hank. He was alone. His eyes pierced the darkness of the room as he stared at me. He lifted his chin, his way of letting me know to follow him before he slipped out the door of the barn.

With the darkness shielding me, I slinked along the wall but didn't make it outside before I ran into Corie.

"Did you see who is here? That's Tatiana, Ricky's old partner." Corie's eyes were filled with tears. "She thinks she can just waltz in here after Ricky is murdered and pick up where she left off in this industry?"

"It is odd." I looked past her with a little anxiety to see if Hank had peeked back in to see why I'd not joined him.

"The way she showed up here. How long has she been in town? Long enough to have killed my brother?" Corie had the same questions I had. "Think about it. She hates me so much because my brother dumped her for me because he knew we were going to clinch the title at the Royal Dance Competition. She knew it. She killed him, which would not only knock him out of a deserving title but get back at me. Then she grabs Sergie?"

"She and Sergie look like they've been partners forever." Not that I knew anything about what it really looked like to be partners for a long time or short time. I just knew they didn't seem like they had one missed step.

"I will not be humiliated like this." Corie pushed past me, and I stood there a moment longer, watching what her next move was going to be.

Once her feet hit the dance floor, it was like her demeanor changed. She pushed her shoulders back, lifted her chin, and with her head held high, she planted one of those big fake smiles on her face and gracefully walked across the dance floor, where she claimed Sergie from Tatiana.

My eyes slid over the floor in search of Dottie and Henry, only to settle on Sergie's dance partner, Di.

It took but a few twirls of Corie by Sergie before Di stormed off, making my suspect list a little longer.

CHAPTER 16

"Sorry it took me a minute to get out here," I told Hank once I made it up to the Old Train Station Motel's little restaurant.

He was sitting at the bar with a cup of coffee.

"Minute? It's been fifteen minutes." He peeled back the cuff of his tux and looked at his watch.

"Part of being undercover is listening and being observant, though it was really Corie who stopped me." I eased down onto the stool next to him.

"Oh yeah. Sergie and Tatiana?" He knew.

"Mm-hmm." I gave a slow lean in and kissed him. "You look so handsome."

"You're beautiful." He smiled, and his green eyes softened. They were one of my favorite features of his.

"Aren't you two supposed to be snooping around?" Mary Elizabeth had found us.

"We are. It's just so hard having a handsome partner in crime." I laughed.

"Maybe you need to stick with the Laundry Club Ladies to

keep your head on straight," Betts said as she walked into the small diner with Queenie, Abby, and Dottie.

"Dottie, what are you doing in here?" I asked.

"It ain't my turn to dance yet. So I came in here to see what my duty is now." She tugged on the leotard's skintight legs, kicking out her feet for extra umph to get them tugged up to her bosom. "Now, I love me some good bedazzling, but this is downright ridiculous." She did a little chest shimmy, causing the dangling beads to shake.

"I think you look fabulous." Queenie couldn't resist touching the jeweled headpiece that came down to a point in between Dottie's eyes.

Dottie batted her away.

"Of course you can't." Dottie's brow rose. "I'm surprised you took off your Jazzercise outfit."

Dottie was right about Queenie. It was a rare sight to see Queenie dressed in anything other than her dance outfits.

"What's the word?" Abby asked.

"I will go ahead and send some of the photos to your email and let you do your thing." I picked the hanging camera off my chest so I could use its fancy digital feature that allowed me to send photos to an email.

Abby was a whiz at all things social media. She would be able to take the photos of the dancers and plug them into her laptop where she worked her magic and find out all the things about all the people. I had no idea how she did it, and I didn't care, as long as it was done.

"Perfect. I'll go on home and get on it. Bobby Ray wasn't feeling well, so I'm going to go check on him." Abby went down the line, giving everyone a slight hug. "Don't forget you need to fill me in on what your big plan is for me."

We gave each other that reassuring look that told both of us that we were good. We were okay, and everything was going to be just fine.

"Tell him to call me if he needs me. You too," Mary Elizabeth said.

"Why didn't you tell me Corie Sadek is staying at the bed-and-breakfast?" I finally got the opportunity to ask Mary Elizabeth.

"You didn't ask, but I told you, all this dance stuff is weird. I've seen her with those people at the Milkery with my own eyes. Odd." She nodded, bringing her hand up to her pearls and running a finger along them. "I guess you think she did it after that little spectacle out there." She gestured to the barn where Corie hadn't been so great at hiding her feelings about the competition taking place. "I talked to Dawn after I got back to the Milkery from dropping you off. We got to talking about Ricky's death, and she said how she was up way into the wee hours of the morning talking to Corie about dancing and New York. They do know some of the same people in New York City. Small world."

"That means we can mark our client off the suspect list." Hank lifted the coffee and took a drink. "But we sure can go and talk to Tatiana."

He leaned back on the stool and put his hand inside of his coat pocket. He pulled out a piece of paper. "Since I have agent status, I have the full schedule of times and places everyone needs to be, and right now, our new suspect, Tatiana, is in her dressing room." Hank handed me the paper to look at.

The times for the dancers to be in place—as well as the times they practiced, could go to the bathroom, took a break, every move they were to make—was listed to the minute on the schedule.

"When Coke had me redo motel room number one as a dressing room for Tatiana this morning, I was wondering what kind of woman had so many requests when her room was complimentary and she should just be grateful." Betts began to tell us about the light-up mirror Tatiana wanted installed and the fresh lemons she wanted—I wasn't sure how fresh the stock at the Safeway, our local grocery store, was this time of the year —for her water.

"Dottie, you better get going," Hank told her since he knew the schedule. "We will all be there to see your big dance."

"It's in an hour. Don't show up." She pulled her cigarette case out of the elastic of her dance outfit on her way out the door. Betts, Queenie, and Mary Elizabeth went with her, leaving me and Hank there.

"Shall we?" Hank stood up and put his hand out for me to take.

"Yes, we shall." I stood up and let him lead the way, dropping our hands so no one would question who we really were if they saw us.

"Room one is what Betts said, right?" he asked.

"Yep." There was a flurry outside—dancers rushing around with bare feet and their shoes in their hands, the ticking sounds of beads beating together, and music filling the air.

Hank gave the door a hard knock, making the star hanging on the door, featuring Tatiana glittered in gold, sway back and forth.

"You better have hot lemon water!" Tatiana's voice yelled from the other side of the closed door.

Hank took that as a "welcome, come on in" and swung the door open.

"You can put it right over there." She glanced at our reflections in the light-up mirror. "Where is the hot lemon water?" She swirled around on the leather bench. "What's with the camera?" She put her hands in front of her face in an X formation.

"I'm the photographer for the Daniel Boone National Park Committee"—not a lie—"and I'm here to get some action shots for the National Park Magazine."

"And you?" She looked Hank up then down.

"I'm an agent for Dottie Swaggert and Henry Bryant. I wanted to let you know I'm thrilled for you and your comeback tour." I watched Hank turn on his charm, and it kinda bothered me, but I just went with it. "Do you have an agent?"

"Depends." She swung her long left arm way up in the air and did some sort of concocted move where it landed perfectly on top of her right thigh. She then ran her fingernail from her ankle to her hip. "Do those green eyes come with the package?"

Ahem. I cleared my throat and started to snap photos.

"Before I take Di on as a client, I want to make sure I am building the right client list and if a certain someone is available." Hank grinned.

I shoved myself in between them and clicked away.

"I think that's plenty." She put her finger on my shoulder and tried to push me aside.

"I have to take candids." I ignored her and clicked away.

"Oh dear. Don't take on a tiny star." That was how she referred to Di. "She's a bit mousey and young. Too bad Sergie feels he needed to train a novice and try to get to the big dance with her. But I see Corie Sadek tippy-toed right in on him today." When she sighed it out, her chin fell to her right shoulder.

Faker. I glared and took a photo when I noticed her eyes staring at Hank to see if he was falling for her drama.

"It is terribly sad about Ricky Sadek." Hank's mention of Ricky made her jerk up.

Tatiana was so conceited, she just wanted to talk without a care in the world and truly knowing who we were.

"I've heard all the gossip around here, but if you ask me—" Gently, she placed her hand on her chest, rubbing it slowly, giving me a look like she wanted me to snap a photo. I did. "Do I think Sergie did it?"

Hank gave me the side-eye.

"Maybe. Probably, though I'd never let the authorities in on how things are around here. It's part of the trade." She stood up, unzipped the side zipper on her dress, and let it fall to the ground.

I looked away.

"Oh, please." She laughed at me. "We wear leotards under everything." She wore a catsuit very well. She put her hands on her hips. "Well?"

"Well what?" I asked.

"Photo?" She laughed and rolled her eyes at me. I took more photos of her, not happily. "If you think about Sergie, he always wanted Corie to himself. When she dumped him for her brother, you could imagine the talk about Sergie not being able to keep his partner happy. I've got to be honest and say that if he did do it, I don't blame him. I was too hurt by the Sadek sibling union."

"How so?" I asked.

"Excuse me? Are you listening in on our conversation?" she asked offensively.

"The camera loves your emotions. The more passionate you are about your words, the more the camera eats you alive." I'd learned in these few minutes that she loved having her ego stroked.

"Anyways"—she flung her head to the side—"you can imagine my surprise when my partner of three years, Ricky, dumped me, of all dancers, for his sister."

"You don't think the authorities will think you had anything to do with Ricky's death, do you?" Hank asked her.

She gave him a frown of cold fury.

"I mean, you weren't his partner. He gets murdered, you

show up. I'm only asking as a concerned agent on how to deal with these sorts of situations." Hank covered himself pretty well.

"Are you kidding me? I just got into town this morning. I've been in Milan for the past three years. I'd not seen Ricky since he showed up at the airport to bid me farewell after he dumped me." She smiled. "I'm glad he dumped me. If he'd not done that, I'd never have taken the teaching job at Dancer International School in Italy."

"You can prove that you flew in this morning?" Hank asked.

"Yes." She picked up her phone from the table and poked it a few times with her finger before she brought up the tickets on the screen. "Have you ever been to the Bluegrass International Airport?"

Her tone told me she was being sarcastic.

"Can you imagine a two-runway airport touting itself as international?" She snorted.

"Imagine that," I murmured and walked over to the door, ready to head out because she definitely didn't come into town to kill Ricky.

"Anyways, I told Corie just today how she needed to check into that crazy dull-haired dance partner of Ricky's before me." She shook her head and went back to admiring herself in the mirror, running her fingertip along her lip line. "Leave your card, and I'll be more than happy to invite you over for dinner."

"I don't have one on me, but I'll be sure to slip one under your door." Hank grinned again, making me 'bout sick to my stomach.

We walked out the door.

"'I'll be sure to slip one under your door.'" I did my best Hank impression when we left Tatiana's room-turned-dressing-room.

"Stop it." He laid his hand on the small of my back. "Playing the part got us some good information."

"Not much. Just that she isn't the killer, and she's trying to look at someone way back from Ricky's past?" I shook my head, knowing this was a dead lead.

"Come on." He took my hand. "We are going to be late for Dottie and Henry's big dance."

CHAPTER 17

Fifi always knew when I was restless. She could never get comfortable and would stare at me until I started to talk to her. I was mostly sure it was in my head, but I really did believe she listened to me, and after I'd confided in her what was rolling around in my mind, I did feel better.

"According to what Hank said about the report where they found nothing in the car, I just don't believe it. Ricky had to have been dragged into that car. There has to be something. A hair. A fingerprint the sheriff's deputies overlooked. Something." I threw the blanket off me and leaned on my elbow to look out the window toward the bungalow.

The moon cast its glow down on the lake. It was a calm night. The lake was still, and all the lights in the campers were off as well as in the bungalows.

My eyes shifted to Felicity and Kirby's car.

"Want to go potty?" As soon as the magic word came out of my mouth, Fifi jumped off the bed and darted to the front door of the campervan.

I snickered and sat up on the side of the bed, where I slipped my feet into my slippers, grabbed my robe, and tied it snug around me.

"We need your leash, a flashlight, and the horn." The horn was for any unwanted critters of the night.

I exchanged my slippers for my boots that I kept next to the door and clipped Fifi's leash on her bejeweled pink collar. I clicked on the flashlight to light our path as soon as I opened the campervan door. With a quick spotlight check on our surroundings, I took the one step out of the camper and started walking toward the bungalows.

"I hope we don't get caught," I whispered to Fifi. Her leash was taut, and when I drew the light to see what she was doing, I realized she was doing her business, so I unrolled one of the potty bags from the handle of the leash and went over to pick up her stinky.

She scratched a few times before she took off in the opposite direction, leaving me there to clean up her mess.

"Thanks," I told her and picked up after her, twirling the bag closed with the contents inside. "Yuck."

She pranced toward the bungalow as if she knew what I was thinking, and I followed her, knowing if someone did catch me looking around the car, I could use Fifi's curious sniffing as an excuse.

"Okay, you stay right there." The command made Fifi sit.

I looked around the car and gnawed on my inner cheek, wondering what exactly I could find. Maybe it was because I was doing something I shouldn't be or possibly the fact that it was the middle of the night in a forest of things I never wanted to come face-to-face with, but the crickets seemed much louder than usual.

Granted, they appeared around this time every year and disappeared during the winter, so it could be I'd just not noticed them coming back. Though they were small, they made a mighty noise. Some hikers and campers would say their noise made the perfect lullaby.

Tonight, they were here rubbing their legs against the sides of their bodies to create the special gift of noise they had. In the background, the resident owl made appearances with his *hoot*ing.

Fifi's ear perked up at his sound. Every once in a while, he made his appearance during the day but rarely.

It was like the owl and the crickets were playing an orchestrated piece, taking care with their instruments. Their collaboration played over the landscape, echoing through the darkness, bouncing off the trees and boulders of the forest.

On a normal night, I would've sat there and listened, enjoying every sound, but tonight, their music caused a shiver up my spine. My eyes darted around to make sure no human was watching, though I was well aware the nightlife from the forest was aware of my presence.

"Okay, Maybelline Grant West," I said to myself. "Focus. Get it together."

I cleared my throat and reached out to open the car door. The ceiling light illuminated the inside. I hopped in and found the switch to turn the light off.

I sat in the dark car and looked around to make sure I was still alone before I turned on my flashlight. I turned around in the front seat and shined the light in the back where I recalled finding Ricky's body. There were food containers and trash all over the floor, which I figured had to have been consumed on their road trip to Happy Trails. Carefully, I leaned over the seat and began to move the items one by one, not sure what I would find. If—and only if—there was something there that the sheriff's department missed, I had no doubt it would jump out at me.

Boy, did it.

Something shiny caught my light for a split second. Quickly, I tried to find the object that had glittered momentarily.

"Dang." I gritted my teeth, knowing I was going to have to get into the back seat like I'd been trying to avoid.

All things dead were fine, but actually sitting or even being within inches of where a body was found murdered did give me the icky factor.

"For the sake of justice." I gulped back my fear as if I were a superhero and climbed over the seat, landing in the exact spot where someone had dragged Ricky's body to be discovered after they'd clubbed him on the head.

I closed my eyes and took a deep breath, giving myself the vote of confidence I needed before I opened them and darted the light around the floor where I'd seen that sparkle.

"Voila," I gasped when the shiny thing glistened. It was a single red sequin, like you'd see on a dress.

Not just any dress.

A dancer's dress.

CHAPTER 18

I sat on the bed with one of Fifi's poop bags dangling from my fingertips at eye level while looking at the red sequin —the single red sequin that I knew deep down was evidence. I smiled, recalling Agnes's prediction about the dancing industry being shady and a part of this whole murder.

There was no way I was letting this out of my sight. My plan was to keep it close, take it to the Laundry Cub Ladies' meeting in the morning, and go from there with our sleuthing.

With the photos plastered all over the dancers' websites and social media, surely we could fine one who had a red sequin dress that we could check out.

I knew for a fact someone did, and I had the proof.

Fifi had curled up at the end of the bed, tail tucked and eyes closed. My mind was racing, and I knew I needed to get some sleep. There were only a few hours until sunrise.

I slid open the small bedroom window and let nightfall curl around me like a soft blanket as I looked out over the drowsing landscape. It was quiet but not silent. The forest nightlife was in full swing. Mr. Owl, the band of crickets, and a family of raccoons had slumped past. The light breeze made the branches of the trees creak. The sounds of popping logs from dying fires around the campground added to the nighttime serenade that lulled me to sleep.

Before I knew it, the sun was shining through, and the noises of the night had given way to the chirping birds of the morning. The sound of instruments and the smell of burning wood floated through the open bedroom window, and it wasn't the usual guitar strumming or harmonica that campers played while making their morning coffee around the campfire.

Groggily, I got out of the bed to see what was going on with the festive, full band music blaring. With my sweatshirt in hand, I pulled it over my head and decided to keep my pajama pants on while I checked out the noise. I shoved my curly hair out of my face and grabbed a hairband from my small bathroom on my way down the hall.

With one hand, I gathered my thick hair and rolled it up into a topknot on the crown of my head, using the ponytail holder to keep it in place.

"Let's go potty," I called to Fifi. She was still underneath the covers and probably sleeping from our midnight snoop fest.

When I didn't hear her jump off the bed, I knew I was going to have to go it alone. Just for good measure, I looked down the hall, and no movement whatsoever came from the covers she was buried in, so I hit the brew button on my coffee maker, slipped on my boots, and headed out the camper door.

Smoke billowed from the few campfires already going this morning. Just a couple of campers were out with mugs of coffee in their hands and blankets thrown over their shoulders. It was that weird time of the year when the weather was chilly or even just plain cold when you got up, but as the day progressed, it would warm up to shorts and sweatshirt weather, only to drop as soon as the sun set. This was early spring Kentucky weather and really one of my favorite times in the Daniel Boone National Forest.

There was something about renewal that I loved. That could be because it was at this campground that I had renewed who I was or because I actually just grew into the woman I was supposed to be and I felt so at home here, a far cry from the condo in Manhattan and the mansion house in the Hamptons.

I followed the music up to the recreational building.

"Once you have mastered the basic footwork, you can surprise Dottie with a fun little turn." Corie's accent had such an excited tone. I snickered because I already knew what Dottie was thinking.

"Henry, your footwork is exactly the same as a basic. However, you'll be leading the turn during the basic then lead into two sets of the basic to complete the full turn." Corie gave such detailed instructions I had no idea what she was talking about.

By the way Henry was nodding and agreeing, he seemed to understand what Corie was talking about even though I was completely lost.

I stood with my back to the other side of the open brick wall so I could listen in without being seen. I had a sneaking suspicion Dottie was enjoying the lessons and the undercover work more than she cared to admit.

Let's be honest. She had a reputation to uphold. There was no way she was going to show her cards in this deal. At least, not until it was over and she had a hand in solving it.

"Now, let's break things down." Corie sounded more like a kindergarten teacher than a professional dancer. "You are going to start with your left. Henry, first step to your left," she instructed him. "Drop the hand, Dottie."

"I'm trying to keep my balance from him stepping on my

toes." I peeked around the corner to see Dottie's forehead puckered.

I drew back and smiled, trying to keep my laugh inside.

"If your feet weren't so big, then they wouldn't be in my way." Henry gave it a good comeback before I heard him holler, "Ouch. Stop hitting me."

"Henry, by dropping your hand, you're giving a turning signal to your partner. Now you're going to continue in the basic to the left. And raise your left hand to turn your partner left together, left tip, right together, right tap."

I couldn't stand it any longer. I had to watch. I slinked around the corner and stood there, watching, unnoticed for a little bit.

"Dottie, before you turn, you will begin with a full basic, starting with your right foot. We have right together, right then left together, left tap. Now you start turning on your next step."

Corie did her best to do the steps alone with an invisible partner as she moved in a turn. Dottie and Henry were so focused on her, they didn't notice me.

"Rotate your right foot out." Corie started to guide them with her hands. "Perfect on your right foot to turn halfway, Dottie!"

The proud and accomplished smile on Dottie's face was contagious. Henry's toothless grin and nod made her glow more.

"Now make another half-turn on your left foot to face your Henry," Corie instructed and headed over to the portable record player where the music was coming from. "From the top!" She gave a couple of quick hand claps before she moved the needle to the beginning of the record.

Corie counted the moves out loud while Henry led Dottie all over the recreational covered porch. "Dottie, keep your eye on your partner." Corie noticed Dottie shuffle a little when Dottie noticed me there. "Remember, more eyes than just your friends' will be on you tonight at the opening of the competition, and these subtle moves will cost points."

"We ain't really compete-in'! It's all for show!" Dottie hollered over the music just as Henry dipped her.

She bounced back up and smacked him away.

I clapped.

"Bravo! That was amazing," I said and walked over to them. "You two are really doing well."

"Just you wait until we spice up their dancing more when I teach Henry to dip Dottie safely and gracefully." Corie flipped off the record player. "Are you two ready?"

"I need me a smoke." Dottie threw a hand like she wasn't having fun, but I knew better.

Corie and Henry knew better too. Both of them looked at me and wiggled their brows, making sure to keep the gesture between us or Dottie would have a fit. Corie took the break to show Henry how to do the new dip.

"Any news on the investigation?" Dottie asked.

I followed her off to the side, where she sat atop one of the picnic tables they'd moved out of the way for the dance lesson.

"Last night, I got to thinking about the car. I just couldn't imagine they didn't find a single thing. In fact, my mind was whirling so much that I wasn't able to sleep." My gaze slid to meet hers.

"I reckon you want me to ask you what you did to scratch that brain itch." It was more of a statement than a question. "If I had to guess, I'd say you took your heinie out of bed and took Fifi for a walk"—she put "walk" in air quotes—"where you just so happened to find yourself snooping around a certain car."

She pointed her cigarette-holding fingers toward the bungalow Kirby and Felicity were staying in.

"And if I had to guess, since you're telling me about this, you found something." She folded her arms across her chest, the smoke from the cigarette curling up into the air.

"Yes." I pulled the baggie from my pants pocket and held it up. "This."

Dottie put the cigarette in her mouth and took a long drawl off it as she leaned forward, squinting her eyes to get a closer look.

"What is it? A hot candy piece?" she asked.

"Dottie!" I shook the bag. "It's a sequin. A red sequin like those kind sewn on dancers' dresses. Don't you see? There was a dancer in Kirby's car the night of the murder. In the back seat, and well, let's just say there's plenty of dancers at the competition who had motive to kill Ricky." It was a huge clue the more I thought about it. A big piece of evidence.

"That place is full of sequined dresses. All colors of the rainbow." She snuffed out the cigarette. "What are you thinking?"

"I'm going to need you and Henry to snoop around to see who has sequins on their outfits. Red-sequined dance outfits." I wasn't sure how to make it any clearer to her than that.

"Were you there last night? You couldn't spit without hitting a sequin, much less a dress full of them." Dottie's observation was right, but one thing she said caught my ear. "What? I know that look. You're thinking something."

"You just said dressful of them. Are you saying none of the men have sequins on their outfits?" I asked.

She pondered for a moment.

"You know, I didn't see any. Nary a sequin on their cummerbunds or nothin'." She got up from the picnic table. "I've got to go. Henry will stand out if he gets some sequins on his suit lapel. And I've got to run and get my bedazzler!"

Abruptly, she stopped and turned back around.

"You know, Kirby could've gone back to the bar like he said and picked up a dancer. They were dressed that night, and now that I'm an insider, I do know they'd made it look like they were doing an impromptu dance. They weren't. It was choreographed months before by Corie. They'd been practicing on their own before they even drove into Normal."

"Dottie! Don't forget to meet me at the Laundry Club later!" I hollered after her. "I'll get the notebook from the office."

I headed into the office for a long morning filled with paperwork, taxes, and new reservations, plus a little snooping of our own. It was my morning to work the office, and since Dottie and Henry were doing the undercover thing, I had to pick up the slack on Henry's end too. But taking wood to the various campers and bungalows was going to have to wait until I did a little in-office investigation. That meant calling Uber was on my list.

Kirby could've picked up a dancer that night, but did she have on something with sequins? I didn't recall any one of them wearing anything other than a black outfit, but that didn't mean someone didn't change later.

And the only way to find out where Kirby went that night was the Uber driver, Barry something-or-other. To be honest, I had no idea how Uber worked. Whenever I'd taken an Uber, it was in the city, and I'd had a friend or even Paul's account. I'd never even downloaded the app on my phone.

"Here goes nothing." I sat down at my desk in the office and put my phone on top, dragging the app icon to life. "Uber," I said and typed at the same time. "Here goes nothing."

I clicked on *Get* and *Download*. I got up from my chair and decided to make a pot of coffee while I waited for the app to install. Instead of jumping on the app that had just been brought to life, I decided to go get Fifi.

I couldn't stop smiling when the first thing I heard when I stepped outside of the office was the dance music. Something told me Dottie was having a lot more fun than she wanted to admit, and it was okay. It was great! I wanted her to find something or someone she could spend time with outside of watching her old crime shows in her camper all night long. It would do her some good to get out and about.

Lights inside the campers were coming to life. There were more fires and more guests outside. The chatter was filling the air more and more the farther away from the office I got. The sound of a guitar strumming along with some claps, laughs, and sounds of plain old good times had drowned out the original music.

The death of Ricky Sedak hadn't touched the guests here. They truly wouldn't probably even know about it unless they'd listened to the local news. And let's face it—when guests came to stay at Happy Trails Campground, the last thing they wanted to do was listen to the news. Heck, they wanted to stay far away from civilization and most electronics when they came here.

That was why I provided as many outdoor activities as I could. We were a few months off from any beach or lake activities, but fishing, kayaking, canoeing and hiking were open for business. It was enough to keep guests busy and occupied so they didn't have to be inside watching TV.

Fifi danced at the door when I opened it.

"Let's go." I barely got the words out before she jumped out of the campervan and darted toward the new smells of the night.

In the morning, I let her decide where she wanted to take what I liked to call her "sniff walk." It was where I'd let her lead me so she could take in all the new smells the critters had left overnight on the tree trunks, grass, camper tires, picnic tables— you name it, and Fifi wanted to sniff it.

"Good morning." I waved to some of the campground guests when I passed them. Fifi had taken the long way around the campground to the office, which took me by the bungalows.

Of course, I craned my neck to see if I could catch any movement inside of Felicity and Kirby's, but there wasn't even a light in the window.

Since there wasn't anything to be seen, I picked up the pace and clapped my hands together to get Fifi's attention so we could head to the office. She knew the routine and took off, arriving at the office door and waiting on me like "What took you so long?"

"Are you hungry?" I asked and opened the door, happily greeted by the warm smell of freshly brewed coffee. "And I need a cup of wake-me-up," I told her.

Her toenails clicked on the floor as she followed me over to the closet where we kept the supplies for the gift baskets and a bag of Fifi's kibble. Then she wiggled her way across the floor to her bowl, eagerly waiting for me to fill it.

"That'll keep you occupied for now, then your belly will be full for a nice morning nap." I poured myself a cup of coffee and fluffed Fifi's bed before I sat down to look at the Uber app.

The app itself was pretty self-explanatory. I didn't see any way to request a specific Uber driver, which kinda stunk since I really wanted the same one Kirby had gotten in order to confirm his alibi.

I wasn't sure when "innocent until proven guilty" had become "guilty until proven innocent by the way of several people snooping into your entire life and finding out where you were the whole time the crime was taking place"—which was where I was with Kirby. Was it not enough that he showed me his ride receipt? Or was it the sequin that I found in his car that made me not doubt his story but wonder if he was covering something up?

After all, it was a murder, and all bets were off on the "innocent until proven guilty" take on the whole thing. The most I could do was explore the app, make an account, and wait until this afternoon to call an Uber to use it.

It took me about two hours to log all payments we'd gotten

from the new guest check-ins as well as fill out a deposit slip and go through the online reservations. Thanks to Abby, we were able to get the automatic reservation details worked out so the guests could pick from the available dates, what camper lot they wanted, and what amenities. Not all campgrounds included all the features Happy Trails did, and that was what made my campground stand out above the rest.

Not to mention, Happy Trails Campground welcomed all sizes of RVs, while some campgrounds only took campers of certain brands or even years made. Yep. If you could believe it, there were campground snobs that didn't let you park your 1980s camper on their property. Not me. Most times, the people who owned those campers were salt-of-the-earth people whom I loved to sit around a campfire and chat with about where they'd been, what they'd learned, and where they were going.

It always made me happy to see reservations from first-time guests. Not that I didn't love and appreciate second- or even third-time guests that had made it an annual trip since I'd taken over, but the expressions of those seeing Happy Trails Campground through fresh eyes lit up in my heart with joy.

"I swear, I'm gonna need some good feet massages from Helen when I get done with this competition." Dottie hobbled into the office right before lunch. "I brought you a pa-ment-a cheese sandwich."

The mere mention of the comfort food made from a simple blend of cheese, mayonnaise, pimentos, and sweet peppers made my mouth water. It was a Southern staple that, after crawling out my bedroom window at Mary Elizabeth's house at the stroke of midnight on my eighteenth birthday to run off to New York City, I was shocked to learn the rest of the world didn't have a passion for like we did.

Utter shock, I tell you.

She put the brown paper-wrapped sandwich on my desk

with a can of Coke and walked on the edges of her feet to her desk before she fell into the chair. Her legs flailed out and arms too.

"Are you okay?" I asked and opened up the sandwich.

The two pieces of white bread were fresh and fluffy. The mounds of pimento cheese Dottie had shoved in between the two slices oozed out the edges, making it easy for me to lick for the sake of not wasting any.

"No, I'm not okay. I still have to go to the motel for more rehearsals. If I'd known what all this undercover was about, I'd never have agreed." She hissed and opened her sandwich. "But I came in here to let you know I wasn't able to get in touch with anyone at the Red Barn when I called to get some idea of who was working the night of the murder to collaborate Kirby's alibi. I reckon they don't open that early, and it was too late last night."

"That's okay. I'd rather you snoop around the dancers and their clothes. I think I'll take an Uber to the bar and try to check all of that out." I really was hoping I was able to get the same driver Kirby had.

It wasn't like Normal was this big metropolis. Of course it had grocery store, drug stores, and a few more shops outside of the downtown area, but I never really needed to go to those stores, though I did go to the Safeway to get weekly groceries. Regardless, I never needed to Uber to any of them. I couldn't imagine Ubering would be a highly sought-after job in this town.

"After I get firewood and check on all the guests"—a job Henry did during the day—"then I'm going to put Fifi in the camper so I can take an Uber to the Red Barn to get some lunch and see if anyone saw Kirby later that night."

"You don't need to do Henry's work. He is doing it then coming to pick me up so we can head down to the Old Train Station Motel together." She must've noticed the grin on my face, though she tried to hide it because she followed up with "We aren't a couple, so get that out of yer head."

She was a spitfire, determined to make me believe her.

"We are putting on a show. Being a pretend dance couple. That's what people do undercover." She pointed to the camera I'd had sitting on the charger since last night. "Don't forget your costume for being undercover."

"Fine." I stuffed the rest of the pimento cheese sandwich in my mouth. "I get the point you're trying to make. But it's okay to enjoy something or someone new."

I opened the office door. Fifi took off before I could even call her name to come.

"You better git on outta here before I jerk a knot in that hard head of yours," she threatened with a wagging fist right before I took her up on her offer with the clue notebook in hand.

The sun was high in the sky, and the day had warmed up. The guests had long gone for their hikes or whatever other activities they'd decided to do today. There were a couple of lingering elderly full-time RVers who loved to sit around the lake in their Adirondack chairs, reading a book or enjoying the scenery.

I didn't dare disturb them as Fifi and I slipped past them.

After I got Fifi in the campervan and made sure she had water in the bowl, I sat down in one of the chairs at the small café table nestled in the kitchen area and opened the notebook just as Hank called.

"Hi there. Any news on the case?" I asked.

"Well, Tatiana was in Italy when Ricky was killed. So she is definitely off our list of suspects. We also had to take Corie off because she was with Dawn like Mary Elizabeth said. I did check with Dawn. If you can believe it, Sergie has been cleared too. Al cleared him before I did. He and Di are actually a real-life couple and sharing a room at the motel. They ordered room service after they left the Red Barn shindig." As Hank talked, I used the pen to go down the suspect list we'd written in the notebook and crossed everyone off but Kirby.

"According to my notebook, Kirby still isn't in the clear. Only his Uber app clears him." I pulled my phone from my ear and put Hank on speaker so I could look at the app on the phone while I talked to him. "I haven't talked to Abby yet this morning, but I plan on being at the Laundry Club late this afternoon, where we will all get together to go over what we've heard."

I used the app to call for the Uber. There was no better time than now to see what I could find out.

"I'm going to go to the Red Barn to see what I can find out about what happened after the big fight that night since Kirby went back," I told Hank, closing up the notebook.

I got up to put it in my bag so I could take it with me. The baggy with the sequin caught my attention.

"Red sequin," I blurted out. "We have a clue! Evidence."

"Evidence? What are you talking about?" Hank asked from the other side of the line.

"Have you eaten lunch yet?" I asked.

"No." I knew he'd say that because it was still too early for him to eat.

"Meet me at the Red Barn, and I'll fill you in on it." Hank's former occupations came in handy as an FBI agent turned ranger turned detective turned sheriff.

He knew a lot of people, had a lot of professionals in his pocket to call on, and just by chance, if he could track down where the one sequin had come from, I knew in my gut we'd have our killer.

CHAPTER 19

"The Red Barn Restaurant," I told the driver even though I'd put the destination in the app.

"Yes. I know. I'm not a taxi," the gentleman said in a snarky tone. "Help yourself to a bottle of water from the cooler in the center."

"Oh. This is my first time in an Uber." I felt all chatty, and from the look he was giving me, I could see I was going to have to rip conversation out of him.

"Welcome." There was a flatness to his voice—and face, from what I could see of him in the rearview mirror.

"I've lived here for a few years now but never taken an Uber. Never had to. Don't really need it today either." His eyes jerked up in the mirror to glance back at me. "I'm a private investigator." I was getting so good at what I was now calling "an exaggeration." "And a client of mine's brother was murdered a couple nights ago. One of the suspects took an Uber from the Red Barn to my campground. Did you happen to be his driver?"

"Does the name match?" he asked. I forgot I could see his name, the make of the car, and all sorts of stuff from the app. "Don't recall."

"Yeah." I shook my head and checked my phone. "I mean, no. Your names don't match."

"You'd be surprised at how many drivers there are around here. A lot of drivers are like me. They work full-time jobs then on some downtime, they might pick up a ride or two." He didn't make me feel any better about finding this Barry guy. "To be honest, I don't even live here. My wife is shopping at some of the little boutiques in town, so I turned on my phone, and there you were."

It was like the air had been taken out of me.

Defeated.

I sat back in my seat and pulled the notebook out of my bag. One by one, I went over the only suspects and motives we had while my Uber drove to the Red Barn.

Corie, Ricky's sister, according to the other dancers, was jealous of her brother's success, and if he was going to go to finals in England, she was going too. The whole sibling-rivalry theory was squashed when Dawn Gentry confirmed Corie's alibi.

I couldn't forget Tatiana. She had motive to kill him because she not only gave him the amazing push to embrace his greater talent by taking him on as a partner when she probably could've had anyone, but he then dumped her after all her work when, like the rest of these crazy dance people, she thought he was going to take her to the top.

When he dumped her for his sister, how humiliated she must've been.

But she, too, had the rock-solid alibi of being in Italy during the murder, far from a stone's throw to the Daniel Boone National Forest.

Even Sergie got dumped during the time Ricky was moving up the dance list to stardom. Only he was dumped by Corie. He had an alibi with Di, and Coke did confirm to Hank they'd gotten room service after the Red Barn, but Sergie could still remain on the suspect list.

Or was he cleared? I hesitated to cross him off.

What if he left in the middle of the night? What if she left in the middle of the night? Did Di have a red-sequin dance dress?

"Here you go." The driver had stopped the car, and I'd not even realized.

"Thanks for answering my questions. So, do you wait here?" I asked.

"No." He shook his head and laughed. "You will need to get another Uber if you need one."

"Thanks so much." I got out of the car, happy to see Hank's truck was there.

The Red Barn was so romantic at night. I'd never gone there for lunch, so this was a real treat.

Immediately, I spotted Hank up at the bar. He was talking to the same bartender I recognized from the night of the fight.

"Hey, honey." I greeted Hank by putting one hand on the small of his back and a peck on his cheek.

He jumped up to pull the tall barstool next to him out for me to sit. A true Southern gentleman he'd become, a far cry from the man I met the first day my campervan rolled into Happy Trails Campground. Back then, he had jumped at the chance to lock me up for springing my now-dead ex-husband out of jail, which then turned into a murder accusation.

I liked this Hank much better.

"Here." Before I hung my bag up on the chair's back, I took out the bag with the sequin in it and handed it to him.

"Fifi's poop bag?" he asked, giving me a strange look.

"No. What's inside." I stretched the baggie with the sequin inside just enough to see the outline. "It's one red sequin to a dancer's dress. I found it in Kirby's car."

"Kirby's car?" he repeated and gave me a disapproving look.

"Mm-hmm. Now, don't you be treating me like that." I told him how I'd gotten ahold of the evidence and made sure not to touch it in case the lab could pull anything off of it.

"Why do you think it's evidence?" he asked.

"Because Felicity sure doesn't look like the type to wear sequins, and dancers wear sequins. What if someone else was in the car with Ricky? A dancer? All of those dancers had a motive to want him dead." I pushed the menu away since I wasn't going to eat anything.

"I'll take the burger platter," Hank told the bartender.

"They all want to go to that huge dance tournament in England. They'd kill for it. Literally." I watched him noodle what I was selling, and he actually bought it.

"I'll take it to the lab. Now, I did talk to the bartender. They honestly don't remember who was in here later that night because they were too busy talking about it, and some of the dancers stayed while others left their stuff here. He said it was a big mess." He ran his hand through his thick black hair. "I feel like we need to move in another direction."

"The red sequin." I tapped on the bag before he put it in his pocket, and we moved on to discuss other things.

Like our cute dogs as well as a new case he'd just gotten from a client not in the Daniel Boone National Park.

"Does this mean you're going to have to go out of town?" I asked. The thought of Hank leaving, if only for a few days, made me extremely sad.

Even though he was sitting right here, loneliness crept up in my soul. The kind like when the darkness of the night hit you like a cold bucket of water. The shock of being alone didn't feel good, especially when you wanted to be surrounded by the one you truly loved.

"I don't know. I have a meeting later with the potential client. It sounds really interesting, though." He nodded a thank-you to the bartender when his burger platter was dropped off.

I should've been thinking about the case at hand, but my mind was wrapped up in the possibility of Hank taking a job out of town, which to be honest, had never crossed my mind. That kept me from talking.

Hank had devoured the burger and pushed his plate away. "That was good."

"I'll ride with you to town. I am going to go to the Laundry Club to go over some of these clues." I knew he was going back to his office in the back of Trails Coffee.

Hank didn't seem to notice my silence on the drive back to downtown. Or even after he'd parked the truck, given me a kiss, and told me he'd see me at the competition tonight.

"He said he was thinking about it." Betts was straightening up around the laundromat after a full day of customers. "Why can't people just throw their used dryer sheets away?"

"I don't know." I moaned, following behind her like a lost puppy. "You're going to have to give me some cleaning jobs if he leaves."

"I have plenty of things for you clean. How about you start by sorting the puzzle station and fluffing the pillows on the couch?" Betts had no problem giving me some marching orders.

The Laundry Club Laundromat was so much more than a place for campers, hikers, and tourists to wash their clothes. It was a truly cozy gathering spot with various areas that made it feel like a home.

It was exactly what Betts said she was going for when she bought the place. She made a comfy couch area with a television up front, a game and puzzle station, a coffee station, and a book nook for readers, which was where we liked to meet for our monthly book-club chats.

She had vending machines as well as folding stations and

those large metal baskets on wheels. Plus, for the business-savvy guest, she even provided a computer.

Granted, it was pretty old, but Abby sure was giving it a go while I helped Betts clean up as we waited on Queenie to show up.

Dottie had already texted to let me know Corie wasn't letting her leave the motel for nothing, not even the death of Corie's own brother. I could only imagine what kind of h-e-double-hockey-sticks Dottie was giving Corie for missing out with the gals.

"I found something." Abby jumped to her feet and did a celebratory dance, making her way over to the couch, picking up the pillow, and pretending like it was a dance partner.

Betts's phone beeped.

"That's Queenie." Betts read the text. "She can't make it either."

"Look. A girl in a red-sequin dress with Ricky on his social media page." Abby kept singing. "Right there!"

"Let me see." I looked at the computer screen at the photo. "It's from six years ago."

"Still. Sequins, red dress." Abby pumped her fists in the air.

I used the old mouse to click through more of the photos and realized they were of the Sadek siblings.

"That's Corie." My jaw dropped.

"No," Betts gushed. "That's Corie?"

"I told you that you needed to keep an eye on that one." Agnes Swift stood at the door of the laundromat, looking so good. She wagged a folder in the air that I recognized as the same ones the sheriff's department used for crime cases.

"Agnes." I rushed to her side. "When did you get out of the hospital?"

"Just a couple hours ago. I called Hanky, and he told me you were here. I promised him I would just drop this off to you and head to get my Precious before I go home to rest." She gave me a gingerly hug while handing me the file. "It has a lot of information you probably know, but I knew Pearl wasn't going to give you anything."

"Do you need a ride?" I wanted her to be safe.

"Nope. I can drive. But you have to promise me you'll come by in a few days after you get that sister in jail." She used a scolding tone on me.

"You look great." Betts walked over to talk to Agnes. "Are you feeling good? What was wrong?"

Betts and Agnes chatted while Abby and I looked over the files. There wasn't anything we truly didn't know, but Corie's statement was vague. She did say she was at the Milkery, but when asked if she left, she lawyered up.

That was something she'd not told Hank, or at least, he'd not told me. You'd think your client would let you know if they called in their own lawyer.

"I'm telling you, these people don't care about blood. We really need to talk to her tonight at the competition." Abby gave me a long, leveled look.

CHAPTER 20

There was just enough time, if I planned it out well, to let Fifi out for a quick walk, feed her, get ready, grab my camera off the charger, and drive back to the Old Train Station Motel for tonight's competition.

I didn't want to miss the number Dottie and Henry had been working on so much with Corie.

"Let's go potty." I didn't let Fifi jump out of the campervan since it was dusk, and that was when the coyotes liked to venture out. "Not a tasty treat tonight."

She waited like a good girl while I grabbed the basket next to the door and dragged it to me. I took her leash and clipped it on her and put her on the ground to lead the way.

"Since you've been stuck inside for a few hours and are going to be tonight, you can take a nice sniff-walk," I told her and noticed a car in Felicity and Kirby's bungalow driveway with the engine running.

It wasn't their car.

"On second thought, come this way." I changed my mind about Fifi taking the reins. "We need to see who is in our campground and if they have a pass."

We did give each guest a car pass for each one of their cars. If they had a guest visiting, we required they check in at the office with me or Dottie. Then we gave their guest a visitor pass for their car. It was a way to make sure everyone was accounted for and safe.

We didn't need any riffraff to bring down the campground that I'd taken so long to build up.

"Excuse me," I said to the closed car window on the driver's side. I could see a man sitting there. "Roll down the window."

"What do you want, lady?" the guy asked.

"I'm the owner of this campground, and I don't see a visitor tag on your dashboard." I bent down by the window and pointed next to his steering wheel where we asked the visitors to put the tag. "And I don't recognize you as a guest of Felicity and Kirby. Unless you're the lawyer."

Of course! He had to be the lawyer Felicity had mentioned she was going to hire for Kirby.

"Lawyer." He scoffed. "Far from it. I'm the Uber driver." He pointed to the Uber sticker in the back window that I'd not seen.

"Uber?" I stood straight up to look over the hood of his car. "Why would they need an Uber driver? Unless it broke down again."

"It was broken down the other night. I reckon the mechanic didn't fix it. I just picked her up at the garage. She told me to wait here for her. She'd only be a second." The man tapped on the wheel. "I wish they'd hurry up. He said they were in a hurry."

"Yeah. The big dance competition is tonight at the motel. But you know that already since you're driving them there." I shrugged.

"Listen, lady, I don't know anything 'bout no motel or dance competition." The driver confirmed that Kirby had gone to the Red Barn to sit at the bar like he'd said. Kirby had conveniently left out the fact he'd taken an Uber to the garage, though he had shown me the app, and I wasn't clear on what I was looking at. There was no time to check the photo I'd taken to see if it said he'd gone to Grassel's. "All I know is she took my name and my phone number down the other night when I dropped them off at the gas station to get the car." His words mushed together in my head. "Big tipper too. So when I got her call about driving her to the airport, I was all over it. That's big money from here."

"Felicity?" I asked.

"Felicity?" He snarled. "Nah. I think her name is Carrie."

"Corie?" I questioned, my mouth dry.

"Yeah. Corie. That's it. Strange name if you ask me." He shrugged. I picked up Fifi and handed her to him through his window.

"What are you doing, lady?" He jerked back, looking at Fifi like she had the mange or something.

"Watch her while I go get your passengers."

His voice trailed off the farther away I walked from his car to the door of the bungalow. "Listen, lady, can you tell them to hurry up? Extra charge for dog sitting."

It was then that I realized all the missing pieces were coming together. Only they weren't missing at all.

The bartender had confirmed some of the dancers had stayed there that night. Even performed a few numbers all glittery-like. The glittery-like had to be sequins. Red sequins. The only person I'd seen with a red-sequin dress was Corie Sadek, in the photos of her brother's social media platforms.

Quickly, I turned back around to go back to the Uber driver. He was holding Fifi out the window for me to take.

"Hold her. Was Corie with Kirby when you dropped him off to get his car at the garage?"

"Yes. They were together." The words barely left his mouth before I ran to the front door of the bungalow and busted in.

"Mae." A shocked and disheveled Felicity stood inside next to some packed luggage. "What are you doing here? I thought you were going to the dance."

"Are you okay?" I asked in a soft voice. "Where are they?"

"Where are who?" she asked nervously.

"It's okay," I assured her. "You're safe with me. I just want to know where Kirby and Corie are so we can get out of here."

I took my phone from my back pocket to call Hank, only to have it knocked out of my hand with the walking stick Felicity said she'd found before our trail walk.

"What are you doing?" I asked her, scrambling to get my phone.

She kicked it away, knocking it underneath the couch.

"Felicity!" I hollered. There was some uncertainty in my voice as I fell to my knees and crawled to look under the couch.

Her heavy footsteps made it oddly clear she was stomping over to me.

I shifted my weight onto my right hand and right knee to twist my body around to look at her.

I threw my left hand up in the air when I realized she was standing over me, about to swing the walking stick at my head.

With a quick thought to tumble, I rolled onto my right side, missing a brunt blow to my head, then to my left as she took another swing, only to miss again.

"You're not going to get away from me. You or that lying piece of..." She let go of a grunt as she forcefully swung at me another time.

She missed as I did a forward roll and popped up to my feet.

"Wait. What?" I rocked backwards with my arms extended in front of me, hands wide open to use them as defense against the stick she was wielding. "I'm confused. Did you kill Ricky?"

"You better believe it. Of course, it wasn't planned." She continued to swing the stick at me, and I continued to somehow evade the whacks as the war waged on between us. "Just like me killing you isn't planned."

The whiz of the wood splitting the air as she swung it buzzed inside my ear like an annoying bee.

With each miss, I could feel her anger and panic rising, trying to go at me harder, faster.

I whipped around the room, skipping, hopping, and jumping to get away from her and that stick. A suitcase fell off the coffee table, and all the contents were strewn on the floor, including a wig and a red-sequin dress.

"Yes. Planning on killing him on a trail did cross my mind before we got here. He wasn't going to commit to our relationship. Do you know what it's like for people to mock you? To have a lowlife of a boyfriend who only puts himself first?" Strangely enough, I did know and I could answer her question but chose to keep my mouth shut. There wasn't anything I was going to say or do to get her to calm down, much less not kill me.

"Where's Corie?" I asked and continued to tilt to the left and right as she continued to aim at me.

"Corie?" She laughed. "The Uber driver thinks my name is Corie. I told him that immediately when I got into his Uber."

"Does the bartender at the Red Barn think you are Corie?" I had to know.

It made total sense now. "When Kirby didn't come home, you went to the bar, and you found the costumes because all the dancers had gone back to where they were staying. You pretended to be a dancer, fooling everyone, even Ricky. He had no idea who you were, did he? But everyone saw Ricky hitting on Felicity." I ran past the wig and swooped it up with my finger right before she took another swing at me.

"Ricky came back to the bar to get the outfits. It was then that I got an Uber for us to go to the garage, where I told him we could be alone." As she recalled her evil moments alone with him, I remembered how she'd mentioned that she wanted her jacket then how she picked up the lift remote and knew exactly how to lower the car, deliberately putting her fingerprints on the evidence with me as a witness.

"It was easy for Ricky not to notice my walking stick, because he's so conceited that he was too busy talking about how great he was." She rubbed the walking stick like it was her baby. "Whack!" Her scream caused me to jump. "Out like a baby. Then I kept him in the car. I started the engine, grabbed the lift button, and sent it up in the air before letting myself out."

Sneaky bird she was.

"If I was going to get back at Kirby for making me look like a fool—and it wasn't going to be that he accidentally fell off a cliff while hiking—I had to come up with a different plan." A grin crossed her thin lips. "Then I might's well act like he was killing someone for making a pass at me. That would not only put him in jail for murder but also make my family think he did it for love and he did love me."

There were many times throughout their stay I heard her say that she should've listened to her father.

She had planted herself in front of the door.

"Felicity, where is Kirby?" When I'd first made my way into the bungalow, Felicity looked out of sorts. Almost like she'd been fighting with someone.

"Dead. Or at least he will be soon." She put a hand to her throat and acted as though she couldn't breathe. "Now I hate it that you have to die too. I really did enjoy our walk about the trees and all that crap. I truly don't care. I only wanted to come here to push Kirby off a cliff."

The door swung open, the corner hitting Felicity right in the back of her head with enough force to knock her to the ground.

"Agnes! Abby!" I screamed when I noticed both of them at

the door, bringing my ten minutes of terror to a close. "We have to get to the garage."

"The garage?"

"Yes." I nodded and grabbed the stick Felicity had dropped on my way out of the bungalow. "Here." I handed the stick to Agnes. "You stay here with him."

"Me?" the Uber driver questioned. Apparently, he'd gotten out of his car and taken Fifi on a walkabout while I was inside running away from a crazy lady.

"Yes, you! Agnes, explain it to him." I darted toward Abby's car. "Abby, I need you to drive me to the garage."

"Grassel's? It's closed for the dance," she told me.

I looked back at the scene. Agnes was on her phone, and Barry was walking back to the house in a stalking motion as though he were on a mission.

"Barry!" I called to him right before he entered the bungalow. "Did you say you picked her up at the garage?"

"Yep." He held the stick and disappeared to his post to watch Felicity until Sheriff Hemmer got there.

"Abby, we need to hurry. I think Kirby is in his car up on the lift in the garage, and it's running."

CHAPTER 21

It was a miracle that we made it to the Old Train Station Motel in time to see Dottie and Henry dance. It was more of a comical routine than an elegant dance number.

Dottie had a big feather-boa fan in her hand, and when Henry would go to dip her, in one quick motion of the wrist, she'd slap him with it before opening it to fan herself.

It was cute how that one little move made the crowd fall in love with them, not caring a bit about Henry still stepping on Dottie's feet. They turned that into part of their routine, and Henry ended the routine down on one knee with Dottie's foot propped up as he pretended to massage it.

Talk about chemistry. They were a hoot and a holler, almost making me forget the craziness beyond the Old Train Station Motel property.

"Oh, Abby! How did you know?" I gripped her hands in mine.

"All of those photos you sent me were somehow hooked onto your phone's hot spot, so the photo you took of Kirby's Uber receipt came through. After we left the Laundry Club, I went back to the library and really took a look at each photo. Then I noticed the phone with the receipt on it was actually Felicity's. It had a pink case that seemed feminine, and remember when she said at the sheriff's department Kirby had picked up her phone? He still had her phone when you talked to him."

I remembered him fumbling a few times with the passcode when he was looking for the app on the phone. I'd thought he was nervous, but really, he didn't have his own phone, but he obviously knew her passcode.

"When you didn't show up at the dance competition for me to show you and I didn't see Felicity or Kirby here, I knew something was wrong." She patted me. "I'm just so grateful Agnes was here to go with me."

"I have no idea how I can thank you." I gave her a big hug.

"You can start by telling me your big plan for my Tupperware business." She took a sip of her water.

"I want you to put a proposal together about how Tupperware is actually good for the environment. By reusing something like Tupperware, it cuts down on materials like paper plates, straws, and all sorts of containers we use at the state-run resorts in all of our national parks." I could see the idea click in her head. "Think about it."

Her eyes started to glow.

"You know me. I'm on the committee, and I'm more than happy to bring it to the table. Then you've got your own connections too." I was talking about all the good she'd done by donating space in the library to the various groups to hold meetings and events. "If you were to score even one of the resorts, that's a start."

"Thank you!" She jumped to her feet and threw her arms around my neck. "You are brilliant! With my marketing skills, I do think this can work."

She gave me one last squeeze before she ran over to Bobby Ray, who was visiting with some locals, to let him in on the idea.

The big band started up, and all the dancers found their way back onto the dance floor.

"Dottie." Henry got her attention. "You ready to dance?"

"Not with you. The gig is up, buddy!" Dottie had shed the dancing shoes and was rubbing her feet.

"I'd love to dance with you." Corie popped up from our table to take Henry up on his offer.

"Does that make you mad?" I asked Dottie, teasing.

"He'll be back." She threw a wrist at them.

It wasn't too long after that I noticed Hank had come into the venue. I waved really high for him to see me.

Abby had rejoined us. Her fingers tapped on the table to the beat of the music between snapping a few photos on her phone and posting them to social media.

"Good news!" Hank shouted over the band music. "The killer is in custody, and Kirby is going to be just fine. They've taken him to the hospital, where he will be monitored for carbon monoxide poisoning. But I have a proposal for you ladies."

Abby, Betts, Dottie, Queenie, and I were all ears.

"Nope. I will not dance with you. No matter how much you bat those beautiful green eyes." Dottie picked up her cigarette case and wagged it at him before she snapped it open to take one out.

"How about a little road trip to a spa? You ladies deserve it." Hank rubbed his hands together while we all squealed with glee. "Only one catch."

"I knew it. I knew it. No man wants to give you something without getting something back." Queenie spoke up this time.

"You're darn tootin'." Dottie pointed to her.

"Now, now. It's just a little bit of something you do best." Hank smiled. "Meddling."

"I can meddle with the best of 'em." Dottie put the cigarette in the corner of her mouth. "I'm gonna go have a smoke." She stood up. "I reckon this tree-forest-therapist business ain't gonna like no tree-huggin' smoker."

Dottie sure did have a way with words.

"I guess we all better get home for some shut-eye so we can get a jump on our new assignment." Betts vigorously rubbed her hands together.

BE SURE TO GRAB RANGERS, RV'S, & REVENGE NOW available at Amazon or FREE in Kindle Unlimited.

RECIPES AND HACKS FROM MAE WEST AND THE LAUNDRY CLUB LADIES

COFFEE IN A BAG

Sometimes we like to jump in the truck with my Shamper hooked up and grabbing a coffee pot was left behind once.

BUT don't fear! We had the supplies to make the perfect cup of coffee.

Here's what you need to bring if you forget a coffee pot or decide to bring less.

Ingredients:
    Coffee Grounds in a Baggy
    Coffee Filter
    Dental Floss

Directions:

1. Scoop coffee grounds into a filter, and then
2. Tie it up with dental floss.
3. Drop it in hot water like a tea bag and just let it steep as you would tea.
4. In a few minutes, you'll have your cup of coffee!

TURN IT UP CAMPING HACK

Most campgrounds offer free WIFI these days which makes it so much easier to use devices when we have some downtime while camping. Let's face it, we used to get away from the world and it's noise by going camping, but with today's technology, we just can't seem to put down the devices. So we are going to have to learn to embrace them.

Though I really do try to not use my devices when Eddy and I are on the road.

Still...here's a neat little tricky saw at one of our stops.

So you're on that family holiday, it's the end of the day and the kids are looking to relax before bedtime. They want to watch a movie on the iPad, so they crowd around it, all trying to hear the same movie. Next time this happens try out this camping hack and see if it makes everyone happy. Grab a plastic cup from your supplies (or if you don't bring these types of cups when camping, make sure you do this time), and cut a hole in the side to fit the corner of the tablet with a speaker. Then sit back and, literally, listen as the sound amplifies.

RASPBERRY FILLED SUGAR COOKIES

Ingredients
- 1/2 cup white baking chips
- 1/4 cup heavy whipping cream
- 6 ounces cream cheese, softened
- 1/4 cup red raspberry preserves
- 1 package sugar cookie mix
- 1/2 cup butter, softened
- 1 large egg

Directions:

1. Preheat oven to 350°.
2. In a microwave, melt baking chips with cream; stir until smooth.
3. In a large bowl, beat cream cheese and preserves until blended.
4. Add melted baking chip mixture; beat until smooth.
5. Refrigerate
6. In a large bowl, mix cookie mix, butter and egg until blended.

7. Shape into 1-in. balls on an ungreased cookie sheet.
8. Bake 7-9 minutes or until edges are light brown.
9. Cool completely.
10. Spread 1 tablespoon of the raspberry preserve on the bottoms of half of the cookies: cover with remaining cookies.
11. Refrigerate for a couple of hours and enjoy!

HIKING HACK

Save your batteries!!

Mae is doing a lot more hiking and she needs to keep things in a backpack to keep her safe. What would happen if Mae got lost and had to spend the night in the dark? I'd hope to think she'd have something like a headlamp in her backpack for these types of situations.

What if her headlamp was accidentally switched on in the backpack and the batterie had died? It would be a mess!! That's what if!

To prevent the button from being accidentally pressed, turn one of the batteries the opposite direction while not in use.

WOW! Isn't that a great idea?

Also By Tonya Kappes

A Camper and Criminals Cozy Mystery
BEACHES, BUNGALOWS, & BURGLARIES
DESERTS, DRIVERS, & DERELICTS
FORESTS, FISHING, & FORGERY
CHRISTMAS, CRIMINALS, & CAMPERS
MOTORHOMES, MAPS, & MURDER
CANYONS, CARAVANS, & CADAVERS
ASSAILANTS, ASPHALT, & ALIBIS
HITCHES, HIDEOUTS, & HOMICIDE
VALLEYS, VEHICLES & VICTIMS
SUNSETS, SABBATICAL, & SCANDAL
TENTS, TRAILS, & TURMOIL
KICKBACKS, KAYAKS, & KIDNAPPING
GEAR, GRILLS, & GUNS
EGGNOG, EXTORTION, & EVERGREENS
ROPES, RIDDLES, & ROBBERIES
PADDLERS, PROMISES, & POISON
INSECTS, IVY, & INVESTIGATIONS
OUTDOORS, OARS, & OATHS
WILDLIFE, WARRANTS, & WEAPONS
BLOSSOMS, BARBEQUE, & BLACKMAIL
LANTERNS, LAKES, & LARCENY
JACKETS, JACK-O-LANTERN, & JUSTICE
SANTA, SUNRISES, & SUSPICIONS
VISTAS, VICES, & VALENTINES
RANGERS, RV'S, & REVENGE

Kenni Lowry Mystery Series
FIXIN' TO DIE
SOUTHERN FRIED

AX TO GRIND
SIX FEET UNDER
DEAD AS A DOORNAIL
TANGLED UP IN TINSEL
DIGGIN' UP DIRT
BLOWIN' UP A STORM

Killer Coffee Mystery Series
SCENE OF THE GRIND
MOCAH AND MURDER
FRESHLY GROUND MURDER
COLD BLOODED BREW
DECAFFEINATED SCANDAL
A KILLER LATTE
HOLIDAY ROAST MORTEM
DEAD TO THE LAST DROP
A CHARMING BLEND NOVELLA (CROSSOVER WITH MAGICAL CURES MYSTERY)
FROTHY FOUL PLAY
SPOONFUL OF MURDER
BARISTA BUMP OFF

Mail Carrier Cozy Mystery
STAMPED OUT
ADDRESS FOR MURDER
ALL SHE WROTE
RETURN TO SENDER
FIRST CLASS KILLER
POST MORTEM
DEADLY DELIVERY
RED LETTER SLAY

Magical Cures Mystery Series

Also By Tonya Kappes

A CHARMING CRIME
A CHARMING CURE
A CHARMING POTION (novella)
A CHARMING WISH
A CHARMING SPELL
A CHARMING MAGIC
A CHARMING SECRET
A CHARMING CHRISTMAS (novella)
A CHARMING FATALITY
A CHARMING DEATH (novella)
A CHARMING GHOST
A CHARMING HEX
A CHARMING VOODOO
A CHARMING CORPSE
A CHARMING MISFORTUNE
A CHARMING BLEND (CROSSOVER WITH A KILLER COFFEE COZY)
A CHARMING DECEPTION

A Southern Magical Bakery Cozy Mystery Serial
A SOUTHERN MAGICAL BAKERY

A Ghostly Southern Mystery Series
A GHOSTLY UNDERTAKING
A GHOSTLY GRAVE
A GHOSTLY DEMISE
A GHOSTLY MURDER
A GHOSTLY REUNION
A GHOSTLY MORTALITY
A GHOSTLY SECRET
A GHOSTLY SUSPECT

A Southern Cake Baker Series

(WRITTEN UNDER MAYEE BELL)
CAKE AND PUNISHMENT
BATTER OFF DEAD

Spies and Spells Mystery Series
SPIES AND SPELLS
BETTING OFF DEAD
GET WITCH or DIE TRYING
A Laurel London Mystery Series
CHECKERED CRIME
CHECKERED PAST
CHECKERED THIEF

A Divorced Diva Beading Mystery Series
A BEAD OF DOUBT SHORT STORY
STRUNG OUT TO DIE
CRIMPED TO DEATH

Olivia Davis Paranormal Mystery Series
SPLITSVILLE.COM
COLOR ME LOVE (novella)
COLOR ME A CRIME

About Tonya

Tonya has written over 175 novels, all of which have graced numerous bestseller lists, including the USA Today. *Best known for stories charged with emotion and humor and filled with flawed characters, her novels have garnered reader praise and glowing critical reviews. She lives with her husband and a very spoiled rescue cat named Ro. Tonya grew up in the small southern Kentucky town of Nicholasville. Now that her four boys are grown men, Tonya writes full-time in her camper she calls her SHAMPER (she-camper).*

Learn more about her be sure to check out her website tonyakappes.com. Find her on Facebook, Twitter, BookBub, and Instagram

Sign up to receive her newsletter, where you'll get free books, exclusive bonus content, and news of her releases and sales.

If you liked this book, please take a few minutes to leave a review now! Authors (Tonya included) really appreciate this, and it helps draw more readers to books they might like. Thanks!

Printed in Great Britain
by Amazon